THE STOLEN LETTER

MARIE WASILIK

This novel is a work of fiction. Any reference to real events, businesses, organizations, and locales are intended only to give the fiction a sense of reality and authenticity. Any resemblance to actual persons, living or dead, is entirely coincidental.

ISBN: 1479312223
ISBN 13: 9781479312221

I dedicate this story to the many way-showers whom I have never met in person, but who have had a tremendous influence on my view of reality, and my spirit. These include: George Green, Bill Cooper, David Wilcock, Benjamin Fulford, Bill Brockbrader, Eva Moore, 'Drake,' Kerry Cassidy, Bill Ryan, Aaron McCollum, Stew Webb, Julian Assange, Bradley Manning, Dr. Steven Greer, Bob Lazar, Dr. Alfred Webre, Bob Dean, Dr. 'Pete' Peterson, Arizona Wilder, Kay Griggs, Laura Eisenhower, Susan Lindauer, Dr. Sam Muggzi, David Icke, Alex Jones, Drunvalo Melchizedeck, Dr. Fred Bell, 'Tolec,' 'Cobra,' Robert Potter, Barbara Marciniak, and Maurice Chatelain. Not to mention the newest whistleblower on the block, (as of this writing,) Amber Lyon. There are many more dedicated men and women waking up our planet, but these are those who have affected me directly.

Many of these people have dared to put their careers and their lives on the line in order to reveal the truth about our shadow government. Others have simply shone a flashlight on the extraterrestrial question. Their truth has become my truth, and it is with the greatest respect, I invite them to read my playful tale.

Acknowledgements

A big thank you to my family members and friends who have reviewed my rough drafts, given many constructive criticisms, and encouraged me to forge on with my first real completed writing attempt. Special thanks go to Jeanne Marie Wasilik, Daniel Westcott, Lynn Monroe, and Angela Crawford. Thanks also to my team at createspace.com, who were always responsive, and did a wonderful job on the edit. I must also thank Tom Bird, whose seminar taught me to let my writing flow. To my writer friends from the seminar, thanks for congratulating me before I made it to the finish line!

Thank you, Allie Gray, for creating the cover!

Finally, a big wave to all my friends in the aol Old Hippies chat, who have kept me company in cyberspace, on many a lonely night.

Chapter One

Suzie liked being the mail lady all right. It gave her a place in the world. She liked reading the backs of postcards from loved ones on vacation to poor goons stuck in her sticky city. Washington DC was perpetually humid.

It had taken her nearly two years to get on as a city carrier. Competition was tough, and the wheels of bureaucracy moved slower than a Mack truck in first gear. First, she had to sign up for the test. Next, she had to wait three months for the notice to come in the mail. Then came the test itself. She remembered that day. She and a crowd of at least three hundred wannabe clerks and carriers stood in line early in the morning and showed their IDs to get in. They sat for the exam in a huge classroom at American University—number-2 pencils, stay in the lines, no peeking, do the math…She'd spent every last minute they gave her, checking and rechecking her answers.

Then, she waited another suspenseful three months for that magical letter bearing her score. She'd made a ninety, with an extra five points for her military service. She thought she had it made with a ninety-five. But in interview after interview, she kept getting turned down in favor of a disabled veteran who scored a seventy-five. That was the rule. She wondered how in the heck a disabled guy could deliver mail. She discovered they were disabled in mind only. And she would learn later that it didn't take too much of a mind to do the job—just stamina and a good memory.

Suzie had mental issues too, but they didn't exactly work in her favor. She'd been honest on the application and told of two brief psychotic episodes she'd had in her early twenties, when she had ended up in the psych ward at Washington Hospital Center. The postal service made her go to a shrink at her own expense and get evaluated. She passed!

About five interviews and one and a half years later, they finally hired her. It was just before drug tests had come into fashion. The nice lady postmaster had asked if she smoked pot. She told her, yes, she had, but it was many many, years ago, in her college days. A little white lie couldn't hurt.

And naturally, she'd had to start at the bottom in the downtown post office. She'd worked the ghetto routes with very little fear. After all, she brought the checks and the food stamps—which were actually booklets of stamps back in the day—so nobody messed with her.

She was thirty-five when they hired her, and by the time she was forty-seven, she'd worked her way up to a route on Capitol Hill—the White House, even. Why, she read the president's mail! Not really, she just watched the letters and magazines go by;

she knew that reading anyone's mail would cost her her job. The first lady had subscriptions to *Southern Living*, *People*, and *Gourmet*, to name a few. And the letters to President Henry Hush were many and varied—some from schoolchildren (handwritten), others from citizens all over the country; many came in thin envelopes from foreign dignitaries. Suzie found it all quite amusing–yet fascinating. She wondered if he actually read all that mail.

One letter that came regularly, like clockwork, every Friday, was rather mysterious. The return address read:

Geronimo Jones
Agloominati Headquarters
666 Pentangle St.
Chicago, IL 60606

It was addressed to President Henry Hush himself, and stamped "confidential" in big red letters. The stationary was exquisite. The envelope itself felt like linen. The return address popped out in shiny gold letters, complete with a bouncy 3-D pyramid underneath. The president's name and address appeared in runny black ink and had obviously been written by a shaky hand. Suzie thought it looked a little sinister, and wondered what it was all about.

Her recently acquired roommate, Chad, had the answer. He constantly warned her of the "insider agenda." The Agloominati was a secret organization that ruled the world. If that were the case, she thought, what the heck were they doing with such ostentatious stationary?

How she had ended up moving in with Chad, Suzie never knew—Oh wait; yes, she did. Necessity, that was it. Her twenty-two-year strained marriage had abruptly ended the previous year when the twins hit nineteen and ran out. Josh and Jenny hadn't just moved out; they both packed their knapsacks and *ran*—two weeks after high school graduation. Precisely then, once the nest was empty, Roth's trickling mental abuse had showed definite signs of turning physical, and Suzie had to get out.

So she hastily answered an ad on Craigslist and ended up on Dupont Circle with Chad. The location was great—just a hop, skip, and a jump to work at the downtown post office. Chad had recently parted with his lover, Ian, and had a room for rent. Chad– your typical eye-catching gay guy with no interest in women. Tall and slender, with deep blue eyes and a blond mop, he was an artist who was in the right place at the right time, selling his paintings to a wealthy local clientele. The best part of the large brownstone was occupied by his studio, where he spent hours churning out his work.

Chad was a very intelligent guy. Ironically, when he wasn't painting, he spent much of his time online listening to Captive Earth, that site on the net with all the insider "truth." Suzie would come in from a long day of work, sweaty and tired, only to be bombarded with news from the underworld. She was informed of how the government was against us, that the IRS was illegal, and that the Federal Reserve wasn't even federal, and was run by cold, calculating bureaucrats who printed money for large corporations and left Joe Six-Pack out on the street without a mortgage. Chad ranted on and on about plots to poison the people with vaccines, fluoride, and chemicals deliberately sprayed out of planes.

He would go on about how every single thing was designed to plunder our constitutional rights; he railed about unfair laws that directly conflicted with the right to free speech, sending those brave enough to expose government corruption to prison without a trial, and violating our right to assemble by allowing the policing of even the mildest of demonstrations. He said that anyone's house could be invaded without a warrant. He cited illegal wiretapping and technology that could look straight into your window and watch your every move.

"Have you read the Declaration of Independence lately?" he would ask. "What ever happened to life, liberty, and the pursuit of happiness?" Oh my, was Chad into it! He was paranoid to the max. Suzie wondered how he could live in such a mind-set and paint such beautiful pictures.

One afternoon in the middle of June, her workday completed, Suzie tripped off the metro, climbed the stairs to her new abode, opened the door, and plopped her purse and her weary bod down on the couch. Chad jumped right in her face.

"They're building a FEMA camp right here in town! Right down the road on Nebraska Ave. in the old condemned high-rise!"

"What the hell is a FEMA camp?" Suzie asked wearily.

"Why, it's a concentration camp, baby girl! They're fixing to lock us all up! Anyone who won't be a zombie for the New World Order!"

"That's ridiculous, Chad. Get me a beer."

Chad whisked off to the kitchen, popped the top off a Sam Adams, and handed her the cold brew. "They're all against us, Suzie. Don't you understand?"

"Oh, please, give me a break! Go back to your studio! I just can't handle all this negativity," Suzie replied.

Shoulders tossed back, his blue eyes flashing, Chad left the room. Suzie had not dared to mention the mysterious weekly letters from the Agloominati to the commander in chief. *Maybe later,* she thought. She downed the beer in two gulps and went to her room.

On her dresser lay the day's mail, carefully placed by Chad, propped up against a photo of her family. It rather pissed her off, Chad handling her mail, but such was life. Some things you just had to accept. "Choose your battles," her sister Nettie used to say. Living with Chad had its upside; she didn't worry about sexual advances. He was as cool as a cucumber toward all women in spite of his good looks—and in spite of their advances. Suzie wasn't interested. She was still licking her wounds from the recent split with Roth.

Roth wasn't a bad man, just a master manipulator. Looking back, she realized it wasn't all his fault. She had never said, "*No.*" She'd put up with all his accusations and fault finding because she'd thought he was right! She didn't know who she was anyway. All those years of Catholic upbringing—she came into this world with a big, black stenciled stamp on her soul: G-U-I-L-T-Y. She fumbled through the mail as she fell on her pillow. *Oh my God, the final divorce decree.* Her head ached. She left it sealed. She threw out the usual junk and slipped into her late-afternoon nap.

▲ ▲ ▲

With a chiseled face like his dad's, green eyes, and a shock of matching green hair that stood up between his natural blond locks, Josh looked the part of a rock musician. He tripped off to band practice, a joint in the only un-holy pocket of his worn khakis. Robert, John, and Josh met Tuesdays and Thursdays in the basement of Robert's folks' place, a nice brick house with a long lawn in Chevy Chase.

"Hey, man, what's up?" Robert greeted Josh at the front door with a slap on the back. He wore his dad's flowery Hawaiian shirt and cutoff jeans.

"Hey, bro," Josh replied, brushing back his hair, a sullen look on his face.

"What's'a matter, dude?"

"I'm glad I'm out of that house of war, but I miss the perks."

When he'd escaped the hell of parental confrontation, Josh had found a tacky efficiency further out in the burbs. He had a beat-up Ford station wagon and a job at the deli.

"Living on your own ain't all it's cracked up to be. Heck, let's jam. Where's John?"

A drumroll ending in a big clang reached their ears all the way from the basement. John, the wildest-looking of the trio, with his dreadlocks and two pierced eyebrows, had already arrived.

The young men assembled in the corner of the blue basement. Robert and Josh slipped guitar straps over their necks. One lonesome music stand held the lyrics to their latest song:

> Peace, peace, peace, peace
> When's our planet gonna ever find peace?
> War, war, war, war
> What the *hell* are we fighting for?
> When I was a child, I watched the butterfly
> Awesome I held it with a tear in my eye.
> I grew up and the world turned mean
> Craziest place I've ever seen.
> And now my dad says, "Be a marine."
> Peace, peace, peace, peace
> When's our planet going to ever find peace?
> War, war, war, war
> What the *hell* are we fighting for?
> American Joe, so proud and so brave
> Hops on an army plane his country to save
> Leg's shot off now he sits in his bed
> Bloody tattered brown children dance in his head.
> Peace, peace, peace…

Josh bolted out the words, headbanger style, backing himself up with the bass. Drums crashed, and the lead guitar screamed. They called themselves the Dead Soldiers.

"Break." Robert made the timeout sign, hands in a T. Soon his mom would be home from the hospital, weary from setting IVs and charting for patients she rarely laid eyes on. She allowed the band practice, reluctantly. Dad was out of town peddling pharmaceuticals.

They sat down on the leather couch and passed the joint.

"We still got that gig at that chick's birthday party?" John asked hopefully, a glint in his eye. "Yeah, man, she texted me this morning." Robert blurted, coughing out smoke.

"Way cool," snorted Josh. The Dead Soldiers would rise again.

▲ ▲ ▲

At 6:00 a.m., Suzie sipped her coffee in the strangely quiet morning. Chad never got up before eleven. She and her coffee meditated, the warm wake-up drink sinking to her gut. *The kids,* she thought, *my darling children, why did I have to let them loose so soon?* She and Roth had both tried to get Jennifer and Josh to join the armed forces—discipline, a job, a promise for their future. Neither kid would budge. She thought back to her days as an army clerk, typing away at the daily dispatch. Sure, it wasn't all peaches and cream, but there was a sublime order to it: first formation 6:00 am, PT at 6:30, break for breakfast, back at work by 9:00, break for lunch at 11:30, back to work by 1:00, last formation 4:30, and then free time until the next morning. People took care of each other—passed the hat when someone was in trouble, shared a bag of chips on duty, offered cigarettes, looked out for one another. *Sure glad they didn't send ME to Nam,* she thought.

Pouring more coffee to go, she crushed out her cigarette, draped her badge around her neck, and bounced out of the door of Chad's brownstone. Another day as a happy public servant. You had to do what you had to do. Survival.

▲ ▲ ▲

Back in Chicago, Geronimo Jones sat behind his large mahogany desk, planning another terrorist attack. The letter from the kingpins was urgent—got to scare the people again. They're getting a little too wise. Instill a little more fear! He grinned as he puffed on his pipe.

Months before, Geronimo Jones had met with a few of his pals from the CIA–Ted and Mac, from Covert Operations Division. They met in a bar in downtown Chicago. Jones was gruff.

"You two idiots, dig a little! I need some Muslims to do this next act. They gotta look good, you know, the terrorist profile. Wanting revenge on the USA, against us dirty Fascists, but more importantly …" His shaggy eyebrows twisted. "…a group that's more interested in some cold, hard cash."

"Yeah, Boss, we get the picture."

Ted and Mac exchanged knowing glances.

"We know some guys who fit the bill. They're hiding out in broad daylight in DC. They're itching for an assignment."

"Fine, then, send them over to my office."

Days later, Anzar and Mohammed showed up in Chicago and Jones showed them the plan. They would require twenty or more fellow "Muslims" to complete the job. The CIA would see to that. They had a pool of unscrupulous, dark-complected rent-a-thugs from which to draw.

"Yeah, yeah, we can do that," Anzar had said. "Show us the money."

They left with a wad of bills and strict orders of secrecy.

These were not your normal Muslim extremists. They were not entirely sincere. They liked their comfortable lives in the States. They knew their religion all right and the politics behind it. They were perfect for the part in Geronimo's plan to burn up the coming Fourth of July celebration. Anzar and Mohammed both lived in Bethesda, a prosperous suburb of DC. Mohammed was a US citizen, having been born in the States, and was now settled with a wife and child. He was a Muslim in name only. His parents had immigrated to the States in the mid-fifties. Oh, he knew the drill all right: pray facing

Mecca, fast during Ramadan, spread Islam to the four corners of the Earth. His parents had taught him well, but he knew they would never go back to Iraq. The government was oppressive, and the customs left something to be desired. When he was a child, his mother wore clothes that covered everything but her face. But as the years went on, she began to dress like any other upper-class American woman. His father, Shafee, held a job high up in the Defense Department and planned to land his son a job there too, as soon as he graduated university. In the meantime, he bought Mohammed and his wife a nice house in Bethesda.

Back in the day, his father would come home from work, stressed out, and yell at his mother. His mother would yell back, "You can't beat me like in the old country. We're in America now. I have rights!" Mohammed knew they were in the States to stay.

Anzar came to the states when he was nineteen, from Pakistan. He missed the beautiful mountains of Tibet but not the politics. He had been a devout Muslim at one time, but he'd been forced out of his home country of Afghanistan across the border to Pakistan, when the Taliban set fire to his town, leaving his mother dead. He only had a vague recollection of his father, who had left them when he was five. Young and ambitious, he owned a restaurant in Silver Spring and had worked hard to enjoy a comfortable lifestyle.

Both Mohammed and Anzar liked their freedom in the United States. In fact, they had adopted a favorite American custom: keeping up with the

Joneses. They had a thirst for more of the green dollars. Thus, they were easily swayed by Geronimo's offer.

The plot was fairly simple, but the stupid chattel would never figure it out. Every Fourth, two hundred thousand or more Americans showed up for the fireworks at the National Mall in Washington. The display would be more spectacular than ever, and at precisely the last moment, Jones's well-paid brown-skinned employees, strategically placed on the edges of the crowd, would shoot tiny sparkly devices into the air, which when they touched the ground would burst into flames—especially when they hit the shallowly buried underground mesh of wires and small explosives placed ahead of time by his police lackeys. Once the fires started, the crowd would be trapped. Thousands of men, women, and children would meet their doom, burning to a crisp. What a barbecue! Geronimo could see the headlines now; he made a note to inform his buddies at CNN: "*Thousands Killed on the Mall at the Fourth*" or "*Fourth of July Bloodbath Leaves Nation's Capital Stunned. Muslim Terrorist Group, Yankee Get Out, Claims Credit for the Fourth of July Attack.*" Serious bloodshed. Serious fear. He and his covert cohorts in crime craved the people's fear. It nourished them like a good meal.

Jones loved his job. He hastily penned a letter to the president—a good time for him to take a retreat to Camp David.

Chapter Two

Chad rolled out of bed at the decent hour of 10:30 a.m., stretching his back like a cat, scoping out his reflection. *Not bad,* he thought, pumping his arms. Pulling on a T-shirt and some loose shorts, he brewed a tea and sauntered to the studio. His painting awaited him.

He slid the landscape off the easel, and there, underneath, lay his latest masterpiece: a portrait of Suzie in her post-office blues, from a photo taken on his cell. She didn't know he was painting her, and he kept it that way. He seriously liked Suzie—though not in a sexual way; her personality rocked. She was so long-suffering, kind and pretty, but alas, stupid. Trudging alone in her day-to-day life, she didn't seem to mind her misery. Why wouldn't she pause a minute from her treadmill life to listen to the truth? He desperately wanted to inform the world, Suzie included, of the darkness coming upon the planet, of the Global Elite, the dark cabal, plotting their moves like a chess game. Why wouldn't anyone listen?

When he tried to tell Suzie about 9/11, how their own government had plotted it, she just laughed him off.

"Common, Chad, our own government killed three thousand people on purpose? You're nuts!"

Chad sighed. Thank God for the Internet. People could find the truth if they'd just dig a little. But most didn't want to. They preferred to believe the media lies!

Even *he* had to forget about it for now though. Suzie was right about one thing: it was negative news. He squirted out some fresh indigo blue onto his palette, poured some turpentine, and dabbed a few shadows on Suzie's face.

▲   ▲   ▲

Jennifer didn't go for all the conspiracy stuff her brother preached. It was her world, and she would believe what she liked. She was an idealist, and she loved her country. She was as pretty as her brother was handsome. Today, she had tied her long brown hair in a neat French braid. In no way did this detract from her beauty.

She sat in the huge classroom at the University of Maryland, watching the lecturer far below point out parts of the human body with a laser. Like her twin brother, she had grown up worldly-wise and inde-pendent. She knew she needed a good job, and she wanted to help people. She aimed at nursing; it was a good paycheck and a match for her talent at com-forting folks. But why, she wondered, did she have to learn all this scientific stuff when all she was going to do was follow a doctor's orders?

Lecture over, notes scribbled, webpage noted, she stood up and slung her sack over her shoulder. Pins and needles struck her feet. She was meeting her dad for lunch. Oh my God, *that* man needed comforting for sure. At noon, she waited outside the college cafeteria. She spotted her dad walking up the sidewalk, his face both desperate and determined. They met with a hug, stood in line, grabbed some trays of mashed potatoes and mystery meat, and walked to a little table by the window.

"What do you hear from your mom, sweetie?"

"Oh, she's all right. Talked to her on the phone last night. She's getting along okay. She wants to have some fool family get-together on the Fourth of July."

Silence. Roth looked excited but grave. He wasn't handling the divorce too well. His whole world had fallen apart. A sailboat adrift in the storm, no rudder.

"The Fourth,eh? A picnic at the monument like the good old days?"

"Yeah." Jennifer sighed and rolled her eyes. "The good old days."

The family split broke Jennifer's heart, but she had seen it coming, read the cards.

"How are *you* doing, Daddy?"

"Just grand, sweetie, just grand; got an empty house for sale, the job's a bitch, and I miss you kids."

Roth worked for a small detective agency, usually following wayward wives or husbands for a price, but not always. Occasionally, his assignments took a different twist.

"Well, Dad, I've got chemistry in fifteen minutes. Next week, same time, same place?"

Her dad nodded.

"You'll be okay, Daddy. You'll be okay."

"Oh yeah, sweetie. I'm a survivor."

He pulled two twenties out of his wallet.

"Here, kid, to tide you over."

"Thanks, Dad." They hugged again, and he left.

Washington DC was an amazing city. All the streets jutted out like the spokes of a wheel with circles interspersed. God help you if you missed the lane for your street; you might be circling for hours. And oh, the beltway! A great big ring around the city. Rush hour was anything but a rush. Drivers texted and chatted on cells; some even read the newspaper as their cars sat bumper to bumper in the evening heat.

Roth made his way back to work, a/c blasting, the news blaring. *"President Hush, in a press conference today, stated that every American has a right to health care. In a related story, Washington Hospital Center and Providence Hospital will be giving free flu shots this weekend only."* Roth pondered another flu shot. He got sick the last time.

High in the top of an old oak tree overlooking Union Station sat Clyde, breathing deeply. His space ride was carefully parked in the branches of a neighboring tree. It was invisible to the human eye of course. And of course, Clyde himself was not visible, or human either—although in emergency situations, he could take on a human form, if he played his cards right.

Clyde was a member of the Galactic Guardians, a group largely unknown to their human counter-parts. They spent a lot of time monitoring dear backward Planet Earth. They intervened in small ways—beaming thoughts, causing coincidences. Sometimes they even averted disasters quietly, using technology unknown to Earth humans. Although people could not see them, they possessed ageless, flawless, bodies, composed mostly of translucent silver light. They usually traveled in groups. Clyde wasn't alone. Gretta and Dorian were standing—er, *floating* by.

Orders from headquarters today were to keep a watchful eye over the trains arriving in the big old marble building below. It seemed some special human was arriving this bright Monday morning with a mission. She might need direction; she might need protection.

Ellery Rocker, a senator from Idaho, had a high ranking in the Global Elite. Her childhood was pockmarked with blood rituals and gory sacrifices. Well trained, she knew the plan. Limit the popula-tion, siphon their funds into Daddy's bank; bring on the New World Order. Oh, there was so much more to it…manufactured hurricanes, phony terrorist attacks, police training, CIA drug running. Round up the dissidents. Control their minds. Keep the state of fear going, that wondrous vibration that kept her and her cousins on the cutting edge.

But Ellery had a problem. She still had a spark of compassion in her heart. She pitied the ignorant populace; she was not so sure she wanted them to meet the doom the Agloominati had planned for them. The spark in her heart kept growing, especially when she took a stiff look at the suffering the dark side had allowed and even caused. She was actually starting to get over it! She hadn't yet, but crazy thoughts of betrayal raced through her mind more and more often. Was all her money worth it? The chateau in Germany, the cozy house on the Riviera, the best accommodations in any city, her insider edge at Goldman Sachs—was it worth it? The real question was, however, was she willing to risk her life?

She just felt too much! She couldn't help the tear in her eye when she witnessed the mother and child on the rooftop in New Orleans get swallowed up and the young soldiers in Iraq and Afghanistan, hot, hungry, and dusty in the trenches of a war whose only real object was to funnel more money into the huge corporate pocketbook. But defection—getting out—that was a dangerous thought.

Clyde was reading her thoughts. *Go, girlfriend!* he cheered from the top of his tree. He wished his superiors would allow him to shift into a handsome man-form, sitting on the train next to her. But not yet. Besides, he might flub it up and turn into an ugly green monster.

Ellery looked at her watch as the train sang to a halt. She had twenty minutes to make it to the Finance Committee meeting on Capitol Hill. They were working on a new tax bill that had some hope—the flat-rate tax. Tax everyone 10 percent of their income, plain and simple. Daddy was dead set against it. Her poor head was swimming. Where did she stand? *Beam me up, Scotty,* she thought. Clyde giggled, shaking the treetop.

She grabbed her bag and her pocketbook, checked her luggage, waltzed out the entrance of the train station, and flagged a cab. She looked stunning in her light cotton black-and-white herringbone suit, with her tall, slender frame and wispy brown hair. She had a funny feeling she was being followed.

A short distance behind her paced Roth. He wasn't really sure why he was following her. All he knew was that he had to record her every move, where she went and to whom she spoke. He caught a cab behind her, and they both raced off to Capitol Hill.

▲ ▲ ▲

Suzie's job was highly mundane. Any idiot could do it. Most of the stuff was trash. Thursday, the packed pallets of newsprint arrived on the back dock. Suzie stacked her bundles on the tray next to her first-class mail. The first-class mail had been shrinking for years, but the advertisers still thought the US mail was a great deal—thus all the junk.

And so it was another glorious Thursday on the mail route. Every Thursday, out came the slick flyer ads, enfolding even more junk. They were a royal pain, and if you flipped them the wrong way, little cards flew everywhere. But rules were rules, one for every customer. Suzie parked the mail truck, put on the flashers, locked it, and got out to walk to the places on Pennsylvania Avenue. Her satchel was full of letters for 1600 Pennsylvania Avenue addressed to White House aides, cabinet members, and, of course, President Hush himself.

Oh wow! she thought, as she fingered the mail in her pouch and recognized the distinctive feel of the letter from Geronimo Jones; the raised parchment tickled her fingertips. They came every Friday, but this was Thursday. They must have hired new help at the mail plant in Chicago! Gingerly, she pulled the letter into view as she walked along. Sure enough, the gold pyramid symbol sparkled in the sunlight. Her heart skipped a beat as she contemplated a crime she'd never even dreamed of. She could lose her job taking a letter home! But she'd been listening to Chad explain the diabolical plans of the Agloominati more closely. She was starting to believe him and all the others on Felix Drones's Captive Earth station. Her head raced as she went through her rounds at the White House, delivering all the flyers, catalogs, and letters to the man at the White House mail desk—all but one.

Heart thumping louder by the minute, Suzie finished her route. She'd never stolen so much as a coupon before! That day long ago at orientation—why, they could fire you for having your own mail in your back pocket! She knew it would be easy though. A little switch to her purse before she reached the office, and that was it. But it didn't slow her rapid pulse.

She returned to her truck, her satchel heavy with the one lone letter. Casually, she hopped back up to the seat. She reached into her pocketbook, which she kept by the gearshift, and pulled out a lipstick. Primping herself in the rearview mirror, she painted her lips and fluffed out her hair. Then, faster than lighting, she slid the letter up out of her mail sack and dropped it into her purse with the lipstick. Her heart raced.

She went straight home, avoiding her usual stop at the sandwich shop. She was a criminal, and she intended to show her rambling roommate the evidence.

Chad was in his usual spot at the computer when she walked in. A video about 9/11 played. More conspiracy stuff, she noted, as the narrator explained how it took more than planes to bring the Twin Towers tumbling so neatly down.

"Chad, I have something to show you," she said, dashing to the fridge for a dark brew. Man, she needed it. Maybe the whole six-pack tonight!

▲ ▲ ▲

Josh couldn't stand his life. He didn't understand the world. At first, he thought it was him, that he was just crazy. Now, he wondered if he was the only sane person left on the planet.

Go to college, get a career, find a job, raise a family—none of it made any sense. Why bring a child into this war-happy, greed-crazed world? And what was college anyway? Just a place to memorize and spit back out the usual propaganda. He didn't believe any of it. He couldn't buy it. He lifted the chocolate milk carton to his lips and drained it dry. He started up his rattle-trap car and proceeded up Rockville Pike to Big Dan's Deli where he made his bread and butter. He punched the clock and nodded at Matt.

"Morning, youngster. Ready for a brand-new day of grease?"

Josh smiled. Whatever. He checked the grill and strolled into the walk-in fridge to bring out the day's portions of ham, cheese, and bread. While he was slicing some tomatoes, his cell phone vibrated in his pocket. It was John, probably calling about the band. He ignored it, remembering the wrath of Big Dan. No phone calls on the clock. Forty-five minutes passed as he and Matt prepared for the lunch crowd.

In walked their first customers. These two guys were regulars. With their brown skin and twinkling eyes, Josh guessed they were some kind of Middle-Easterners but they seemed pretty acculturated. They ordered their usual veggie wraps and took a seat in a far corner of the dining room. They spoke in hushed tones.

"Looks like we've got our work cut out for us, eh, friend?" said Anzar.

"I sure hope it won't interfere with my college; engineering is looking better every day," Mohammed replied.

"You won't make this kind of dough being an engineer, son," replied Anzar. "A million each for a day's work; man, I'm taking a vacation as soon as we do this deal."

"Yeah, our brothers back home will be proud of us. I *guess*." But Mohammed was not so sure.

"What about the explosives he was talking about; do we have to set them up too?"

"Naw," replied Anzar, "Jones has got some of his electrical guys to do that. All we have to do is throw those special sparklers in the air and arm our backup guys with some."

"We don't have to provide the back-up guys, right?" said Mohammed.

"No," replied Anzar, "and it's a good thing too—I'd be embarrassed to ask any of our

brothers down at the Mosque."

"But what about the police?"

"Geronimo's got that figured out too—the word for the cops is to look the other way."

"But what if some rookie decides to be superman for a day?"

"Good point, Mohammed. Good point. We'll be taking our chances."

▲　▲　▲

Chad hardly noticed Suzie walk by, let alone heard her. He was madly engrossed in a Felix Drones video all about the mysterious concentration camps popping up all over the country, many in deserted military bases and strategically placed near railroad tracks. It showed pictures of rows and rows of hard plastic coffin-sized containers, stacked up on each other like Dixie cups, with huge stacks of lids beside them. The cameras didn't get too close to the shiny new box cars, but according to Felix, there were chains welded into the walls. *Incredible,* he thought, *they really are out to get us!* Who in the heck were the prisoners meant to be, clamped inside these curious rail road cars? You and me, according to Felix—all of the peons who refused to toe the line for the New World Order, who refused to be controlled.

"Chad, did you hear me?" Suzie's heart was still racing.

"Huh?" Chad looked up.

"I *said* I have something to show you!"

She pulled the evidence out of her purse—the letter from Geronimo Jones to President Henry Hush.

Chad leaned back in his chair, glancing at his work-worn roommate.

"You should watch this video, Suzie. It's incredible! All about FEMA camps!"

"Chad!" Suzie shouted. "This is important! This is right now!"

"Okay, okay, let's see what you've got."

Chad took his eyes off the computer screen and rolled his chair around. She handed him the letter, still sealed. "Where the *hell* did you get that?"

Then he put two and two together.

"Oh my *Gawd*, Suzie! You're risking your job here! You stole a letter? Addressed to the *president*?"

Suzie slid low on the couch, fumbling at her beer, and then downed the whole bottle.

"Hey, pretty boy, you helped."

"What do you mean I helped?"

"Listen, Chad, I'm starting to believe all your conspiracy theories! Look who it's from!" She pointed at the gold pyramid and the return address. "And besides, I'll deliver it tomorrow anyway; no one will know. It came a day early; they usually come on Friday."

Suddenly, their eyes locked. They knew what they had to do.

Chapter Three

Ellery whisked out of the cab in front of the Capitol, handing the cabbie a twenty-dollar bill. "Keep the change," she said, as she hurried along to the committee meeting. Clyde, invisible but clinging to the cab's lit sign, slid down and followed. Roth's cab rode close behind; he hopped out and followed the pretty lady, but his mind was somewhere else. He was thinking about the Fourth of July, the celebration coming, and the possibility of a brief family reunion. It made his head ache. He switched gears walking up the steps of the Capitol, wondering where Ellery would lead him.

▲ ▲ ▲

Meanwhile, Clyde was getting signals from space. "Yes, keep this girl in your sights, but we have other important assignments. You may need reinforcements."

When Clyde was not lowering his vibration to come to Earth, he was actually an angel of sorts. He was from the planet Zandbia, where all beings lived in perfect peace, where millions of his interstellar friends from there and other planets communicated without language or cell phones and the technology was so advanced they could travel light years in a day. So what was the draw from Mother Earth, a tiny planet whose human inhabitants seemed bent on destroying themselves?

The point was the Universe was a whole living, breathing being. When a part of it was sick, the whole system suffered. Clyde and the other benevolent aliens wanted to help. In fact, they *did* help, in many unseen ways. Trouble was, they usually could only work with humans who thought outside the box.

The Finance Committee droned on, as Ellery tried to keep her eyes open. Before they ever got around to the tax issue, a list a mile long about military expenditures came before them. Ellery's normal stance was to vote as much cash as possible into the military budget, doing as she was told. But now her mind grimaced, thinking about the photos she'd seen on the Net of troops sleeping in mud holes and of soldiers sent home to Walter Reed, their brains and bodies blasted. "Don't you think we could trim a little of that off and give it to education?" she found herself chiming in, surprising both herself and her elders on the committee. A stern glance from Senator Conart took her breath. "Oh, I was just thinking," she said and then straightened her hair and crossed her pretty legs.

Roth had been allowed in, along with a few other spectators who actually gave a darn about where the money went. He wondered why he was watching this girl at all.

▲ ▲ ▲

They both knew what they had to do and that they had to do it carefully without so much as a wrinkle or a tear. Chad poured some water in both a saucepan and the teakettle. They would see which one worked better. Suzie's forehead beaded with moisture, and it wasn't from the steam.

"Let me handle this," said Chad, seeing her nervousness.

"Okay."

Suzie knew that Chad would do a better job of unsealing the letter. He was precise and patient. "Get me that metal palette knife from my studio. And clean it off."

"Okay, okay." Suzie did as she was told. When she came back into the kitchen, there stood Chad, gently holding the precious letter in tongs above the steaming saucepan.

"Okay, palette knife, please," commanded Chad, like a doctor in surgery. Ever so gently, he broke the seal. Their eyes locked again in disbelief and suspense.

This better be worth it, Suzie thought, as Chad gently pulled the letter out of the envelope with a pair of tweezers. He laid it carefully on the kitchen table, and they both read:

Dear Prez:

Orders from headquarters: We are planning a little shake-um-up for the peons soon. You know the drill: act surprised; blame it on the terrorists. This might help us get that RFID chip thing passed. Advise your people: Don't attend the 4th of July fireworks. It's going to get really hot. Burning hot. More details later.

So mote it be ~~ GJ

A quizzical look crossed Suzie's face, and Chad raised his eyebrows. What could this mean? A plan in the works regarding the Fourth of July celebration in DC?

"Darn it! He could've been more specific!" Suzie said. "I don't think I can get away with this twice." Chad scratched his head.

"We've got to get the word out, my dear—warn the people."

"Oh yeah, right, who's going to believe us? And besides, what about me?"

Suddenly, Suzie was struck with a massive blow of paranoia. She didn't know she had so much fear in her heart. There went her pulse again, up over a hundred. *Oh my God,* she thought. *What if they find out I did it?* Her job was at stake. Her very life was at stake. Folks fell off the planet for less. She'd been taught all her life to toe the line. Don't make waves. Things go better when you keep your mouth shut. Suzie had done a good job of it, keeping her opinion to herself, enclosed in a shell of phony loyalty to the status quo. Now she was petrified to the bone. Chad gently gave her the letter back, resealed and looking fresh. He'd made a copy with his printer. "Here you go, sweetie, all set to deliver tomorrow. Don't sweat; it's going to be all right." Suzie had gone numb. She was smoking a bowl now as she clung to her Sam Adams. *Go to sleep; wake up; go to work; make a plan,* she thought to herself. She set the alarm and dropped into a deep slumber.

▲　▲　▲

"I don't care if it rains or freezes, long as I've got my plastic Jesus, sitting on the dashboard of my car." Jennifer found herself humming the silly song that her mother used to sing. *"I don't care if it's dark or scary, long as I've got my Virgin Mary..."* Today was going to be a good day. She felt alive, and the campus was huge. She had a long bike ride from the dorm to her class, but the air was crisp and clean and she was on her way. She liked being on her own. No, she didn't miss it a bit, the huge arguments between her mom and dad, the constant state of tension. Now she was free to be herself; she didn't have to edit her behavior to please a couple of lunatics!

She liked psychology. She liked figuring out what made people tick. By then, she was settled in her seat in a class of three hundred, her book opened to the bit about Pavlov's dog.

It was the middle of June, and her summer school classes were so very concentrated. She spent her life in the library and online just to keep up. Now her thoughts wandered to the coming Fourth of July. What was it her mother had in mind? A picnic at the mall! Maybe she could find a friend to come along to diffuse the tension.

▲ ▲ ▲

In a plush underground conference room, many layers beneath the Capitol in Washington DC, a group of very special planners held a very special planning meeting. It was not open to the public. In fact, it was very private indeed. But they didn't need a "Private— Keep Out" sign on the door because only the very special planners knew of the very special room's existence. Delicious Brazilian coffee was served, and ashtrays were set out for the smokers. Some of the brothers still smoked, and this was not a problem.

Beneath a gray cloud of aromatic cigar smoke, at the head of the table, sat Geronimo Jones himself, a stack of printed handouts in his nonsmoking hand. Around him sat a superior group of handsome, hand-picked individuals, who knew in their hearts that whatever the dire temporary consequences were, they would truly save this overpopulated world. They didn't see themselves as the "dark cabal," as some outsiders called them. They were after the interests of the whole world and their own as well. There was no difference.

To Jones's right sat President Hush, and around the table were many other important faces—the secretary of state, the CEOs from the major news media, and the head of the Federal Reserve. At the far end of the table sat the pristinely dressed Ellery Rocker. She alone had some doubts knocking around in her head. She hid them well.

The meeting wouldn't be complete without a showing from the Galactic Guardians. Only their tall, light-filled bodies weren't showing at all. Clyde hovered behind Ellery; his friends Gretta and Dorian perched in opposite corners of the ceiling. They all tuned in and waited for the meeting to begin.

"All rise for prayer!" boomed the deep, dark voice of old man Jones. Immediately, the group stood up and began to recite,

"Lucifer, thou Mighty Master,
Whose streets are paved with alabaster,
Keep us on our humble way.
Your will be done,
You light the day."

"So mote it be," mumbled and rumbled around the room as the privileged few sat down to get the latest scoop from Jones.

"Ladies and Gentlemen, welcome. As you are well aware, the chattel are getting a little out of hand. They are becoming too aware of our plans. This, of course, was *not* part of the plan! So a little intervention is in order. The usual weapons—confusion, intimidation, and fear—that always work so well. This time, the setting will be the DC Mall on the Fourth of July during the fireworks celebration. The plan is an attack by Muslim terrorists. We have a group ready and willing to do the job. They will shoot special sparklers into the air, during the smashing grand finale. Already set are some underground explosives, easily triggered by the sparks. The result will be mass mayhem and death. Even more casualties than 9/11, and the shock will be fantastic! Our friends at CNN, NBC, ABC, CBS, the *Post*, and the *New York Times* already have the story." He nodded at the press. "Here is a little rundown of the plan."

The coffee girl, dressed in a very short black-and-white maid's outfit, passed out the handouts and poured fresh coffee. She smiled very politely as she served her elite clientele, but she seemed to be in a trance. Jones's eyes followed her.

"Just remember, folks, we need you. Don't be a casualty. Stay away from the Mall on the Fourth."

He wacked the coffee girl's behind.

"So mote it be, folks! This meeting is adjourned."

The room broke into a sea of voices as the brothers and sisters caught up on the latest news in their personal lives.

Ellery glanced at the handout, slid it into her briefcase, and stood up. Her eyes met Abel's. He was her friend from the press from long ago. Out of sight he'd been, but not out of mind. She'd never forget that day he'd had his way with her in, of all places, the men's room in the Capitol building. Now a shock wave traveled up and down her body as his eyes cased her head to foot. And to think that day he'd gone straight into the press conference all non-chalant like nothing had happened. She smiled back across the room, picked up her bag, and left. She knew there would come another chance to dance. But it could wait; she had to get back to her commit-tee meeting.

▲ ▲ ▲

Roth couldn't figure out what had happened to Ellery. He thought he was losing his mind. Surely he would lose his rent-a-cop job if he didn't figure this one out. She had just plain vanished! What the heck good was this high-dollar mini-camera pen going to do if he lost his charge? She'd excused herself from the Finance Committee meeting, saying she'd be right back, and she clacked-clacked her pretty high-heeled feet into the ladies' restroom. He should have known something was fishy when she carried her briefcase along. But he *knew* he saw her going in, so he waited. And he waited. After a half hour, his eyes fixed upon the heavy, carved brown wood door, he took a chance. No one was watching. Gingerly, he backed into the bathroom door. *Wow, much neater than the men's room,* he thought. It was quiet. It was *empty*! It couldn't be empty! His eyes hadn't left the door since Ellery had stepped in! He looked for a back entrance. None. He pushed in the door of every stall. Not a soul. He tiptoed back out into the grand hallway.

To keep up appearances as Mr. Joe Blow American Citizen, who actually cared about where his money went, he walked quietly back into the committee meeting, pen and notebook in hand. He sat down, discouraged and bewildered.

Another rather boring half hour had passed, during which he'd witnessed figures too large to imagine—a hundred million here, two hundred million there—when in walked a slightly disheveled Ellery. "I'm very sorry, Senator. I had an important call on my cell."

"Not to worry, Miss Rocker, we haven't voted yet."

"Oh good," she said, ducking down into the desk she'd left behind, as the chairman continued his monotonous drone. *Well, at least she's back,* thought Roth as he shifted on his bench, propping his pen up to his nose in phony thought and taking her picture. He could swear she smelled like coffee.

Now, even Ellery looked bored. Here it was almost an hour later, and they seemed no closer to a vote. Roth watched as she pulled some paperwork out of her briefcase and scanned it; her eyebrows arched. Click, click, click.

Chapter Four

Josh loved band practice. It got his mind off his so-called life. *Nothing like just sinking into the music,* he thought. They had to get a song lineup for Mary Candy's birthday bash, which was coming up in just a few weeks. She was turning sweet seventeen June 29, and her parents had money. Josh could use a little extra green right about now.

The blue basement of Robert's parents' house was still the same and somehow comforting to Josh. Oh, he knew he'd needed to leave home when he did, but he had left behind a measure of security. Brushing a long lock of blond hair away from his forehead, he picked up his bass. John rolled the drums, low and loud. Robert twisted the pegs on the neck of his guitar, tuning up. Another young group of unknown rebels sang into the waiting summer breeze. They may not be famous, but their thoughts mattered, didn't they?

▲ ▲ ▲

For sure their thought waves mattered. Clyde and his two companions, Gretta and Dorian, knew this all too well. They were waiting for the humans to catch up, and it was taking an eternity. You see, the Galactic Guardians needed more than zero-energy fuel to keep them and their spacecraft moving. They were propelled and likewise delayed by the thoughts of their human counterparts. Only a small percentage of the Earthlings realized the power of their thoughts. It was this 7 percent, the diamond hearts, thinking good thoughts, and inviting help from above, that gave them permission to interface at all in the lives of men.

They were having a post-meeting conference at the Lincoln Memorial steps—invisible to humans of course. All three had photographic memories, and each was dismayed at the plans of Geronimo Jones and Co.

"Well, I guess we'll need a counterplan," said Gretta.

"Duh!" replied Clyde.

"But don't we have limits?" asked Dorian. "Like… you know…like we can do a lot more when requests are made?"

"You're thinking of Archie Mike and the Angels; they *really* have to wait for human orders! But we've got a little more leeway—at least more than we used to."

"Well," said Clyde, "we must have both a prevention plan and a counterattack."

His friends nodded.

"There's not a whole lot we can do with Anzar and Mohammed, their minds are set. And I don't think Source Captain will allow us to disable their weapons," said Gretta.

"I guess it's really up to Suzie, Chad, and Josh. The ball's in their court," said Clyde.

"Right. This is a free will planet after all, and we cannot force anything," said Dorian as Gretta nodded.

"Well then, so much for any direct intervention on our part," Clyde shrugged.

The small group of invisibles chatted on, plotting. The birds could see them and gathered at their feet. A small child in a stroller pointed and screamed with delight, "Look, Mommy! Look, Mommy!" as the birds scattered.

The mother replied, "Yes, dear, how pretty."

▲ ▲ ▲

The downtown post office hummed with the bustle of clerks, carriers, and customers. The carrier area, out of view from the customers, looked like a maze of three-sided cages, each holding a letter carrier in a blue uniform. This was where they got their mail in order, ready to take to the street. Suzie stood at her post, sliding magazines into place in the order of her route, a fresh Styrofoam cup of coffee nestled between the newspapers that lay before her. How the other carriers held a conversation while they cased their mail, she'd never know. It took all her concentration and brain power just to get her mail ready to go, which of course didn't stop the chatter of her thoughts. She had a half-baked plan in her head to gather her broken family together on the Fourth. She had put the word out to Jennifer and Josh, who would surely tell their father, but this was before she'd read the letter from Geronimo Jones. *You idiot, what's the point anyway? You absolutely loathe Roth,* said one of the many voices in her head. *And now that you know, what's the point of putting them all in danger for a silly family tradition?* added another dissident voice. Sometimes she wished that a trapdoor would open in the floor and she could totally disappear, or that she could just go to sleep for a thousand years. This life was just too damned hard.

"Miss Striking," a voice behind her interrupted her thoughts. It was her supervisor, Jane Doright. "Mr. Elliot would like to see you in his office right away."

Now her head was really screaming! *Good Gawd, how could they have found out?* But she kept her cool, her face not showing the terror in her heart. She picked up her coffee cup and headed to the postmaster's office.

She sat down in the gray metal chair next to his desk, ready to deny everything.

"Miss Striking, you've always been a willing worker, and without a doubt, your customers rave about you."

Suzie smiled and sipped her coffee, as her heart dropped to her feet. *Here comes the hammer,* she thought as she smiled up at her boss.

"I know you put in for vacation the days before and after the Fourth, but I could really use you. Since

Patrick broke his leg and Danny had the shepherd attack, we've been really shorthanded."

"Oh, I see," answered Suzie, doing her best to look disappointed as every cell in her body flooded with relief. "So you need me to fill in a few days?"

"Yes, if you don't mind, Miss Striking."

"No problem, Mr. Elliot. I could use the extra cash, and I'll just save up my vacation days."

"Okay, I'll put you on the schedule then. Have some fresh coffee."

Suzie poured herself some more coffee from the postmaster's personal coffeepot and floated back to her case, walking on air.

"What did the old codger want this time?" asked Sally from the next case.

"Oh, I got to work around the Fourth is all."

"Bummer, Suze."

"Hey, I'll live through it."

And indeed, she would, thought Suzie, as she got back to her cubicle and her private ponderings. *Good grief, that was a close one! Thank you, God, if you're up there! Solves my Fourth of July dilemma too. I'll just tell the kids I can't make it. Have to work early the next day.*

▲ ▲ ▲

But Roth, her unhappy ex and the father of her children, already had a plan. The more he contemplated a little family gathering for old time's sake, the more he liked it. He and his ex and the kids with a picnic basket full of peanut-butter-and-jelly sandwiches and pink lemonade. The fireworks at the National Mall, just like old times!

▲ ▲ ▲

Another lunch with Dad. It made Jennifer feel so sad. Her once cocky, know-it-all father was now a jittery nervous wreck. It used to be Mom who was the jumpy one. Oh well, she could endure it; after all, he was her dad and he meant well. She waited at the entrance to the student union cafeteria standing still, as the throng of future graduates hustled toward the food. She spied him. Handsome but worried, a black shock of hair in his brown eyes, Roth trudged up the cement stairs, no spring in his step—until he spied his daughter. At once, he smiled and his walk lightened.

"Hey, Daddy-O, how you been? You look nice. What's with the suit?"

"I have a new assignment, kid. What's up with you? You acing all your classes?"

"I'm trying to, Dad. Hey let's get some vittles."

They got in line; each grabbed a white plastic tray and knocked it along the steel railing, gathering up the plates. Roth paid the bill, and they found the only booth left.

"So what do you hear from your mom, sweetie? Are we still on for the Fourth?"

"I dunno, Dad. Mom called last night and said she had to work the fifth and didn't want to stay out that late. So I guess no family picnic." Jenn sighed, trying to hide her relief.

"Well, that doesn't have to keep you and your brother and I from getting together, does it, hon?" Roth had rarely organized family outings; in fact, he had usually thought up an excuse to skip. But now, he wanted desperately to nurture the fragile connection that still remained with the twins.

Jennifer was flummoxed! She couldn't believe this was her dad talking. She nervously scratched the pages of her closed microbiology book, scraping out a rhythm.

"Well, uh, I suppose, Dad."

"Let's do it, kid! You and me and Josh—hey, bring a friend if you like. Pack up a little picnic for us, hon, eh? We can all meet in Takoma Park and take the metro in. I'll call your brother tonight. It's just next week, ya know. Whadya say, kid? We got a date?"

With a crooked smile and a shrug, Jennifer said, "We'll see the lights, Dad. We'll go see the sparkly lights," echoing her childhood words, traveling back in time.

Chapter Five

The Washington DC Department of Parks and Recreation—not to mention the police and the firemen—had their work cut out for them every year on July 4. Permits had to be signed, skilled pyrotechnicians assigned to setting off the display, positions planned for the police. No one seemed to notice how tired Chuck and Al were, the lowly janitors of the crew. They'd been up the past two nights digging thin trenches in the grassy Mall and filling them with slender wires. By the time they were done, they had a network like a checkerboard up and down the huge soon-to-be picnic area. Captain Bob Mason, the chief of police, had directed them. He said the wires were a surveillance device, a way to deflect possible terrorists. The wires and the little black cylinders were carefully buried every one hundred yards or so. They looked like little bombs. Al dismissed the thought. What did he know? He and Chuck got double time for planting the little boogers. Captain Mason had said to tell no one. Hey, the money was worth it. They could afford a case of *good* beer next Saturday!

Chief Bob Mason knew better. He knew those wires were not surveillance devices. He also knew he'd get a promotion at the Lodge.

▲ ▲ ▲

Roth liked e-mail—especially since it allowed him to escape direct contact with Suzie, by phone or in person. He still had this nagging feeling he'd done something wrong, but he couldn't place it. What he did know for sure was that his ex was none too friendly these days—barely cordial in fact. He carefully chose the words as he typed:

What are your 4th of July plans? The kids said something about a picnic at the Mall.

Thanks, Roth

He knew she had to work the next day, but she didn't know he knew. Maybe she would come anyway. Heck, he could make the sandwiches this year.

He heaved a heavy sigh and clicked send. Now back to work. He slipped the little SD adapter card out of his magic camera pen into a small port in his laptop. Time to see what his slender senator was up to. The first shot showed a bored and almost sad Ellery. What was so important about her anyway? Why was he following her? What he didn't know was that her own father, John D. Rocker, a kingpin in the Global Elite, wanted to make sure she wasn't stepping out of line.

Shot one, just some papers. Shot two, Ellery leaving the capitol building and catching a cab. "Highly suspicious," mumbled Roth as he flipped back to the picture of the paperwork on her desk that day. Boring Finance Committee stuff, no doubt. But something caught his eye: a little pyramid with rays going out, up in the left-hand corner of the paper. He zoomed in on it.

Welcome, Ladies, Gents of Light!
We'll make it thru the cold, dark night!
Nothing can stop our lofty fight.
To free our world from Pain and Fright.
Lucifer He stands alone,
Our world's illness to atone!
~~So mote it be~~

Then a faint scribble: July 4—terrorist attack?

Roth's dark eyebrows furrowed. What was *that* all about? That surely wasn't a list of expenditures to be approved by the Finance Committee, which was on the agenda the day he took the picture. Had Ellery gone down some rabbit hole to fantasy land? And what was that strange sketch on the bottom? It looked like a bomb with a fuse. What was Ellery up to? Was she a member of some secret cult? Was that why he was following her?

It was late, time to go home. He was tired; he checked his e-mail. No response from Suzie.

▲ ▲ ▲

Ever since she and Chad had opened that letter, Suzie's stomach had been tied in knots. Another Friday had passed; another letter with the bright-gold pyramid went through her hands and on to the White House mail desk. She didn't dare confiscate that one. She'd pressed her luck far enough.

Her thoughts raced as she made her short journey home from work. What did it all mean? Were the Agloominati *really* planning something for the Fourth of July? Chad had been on her back day and night. He wanted to go on YouTube and warn the people. He wanted to call Felix Drones at Captive Earth. Suzie would have none of it. She tried to block it all out. She didn't want to lose her job. But a little voice kept saying, "What good's your job if you're fried meat, huh?"

"Sicko," she answered herself.

The little voice retorted, "Don't be sorry, Suzie. Think ahead."

And there was that e-mail from asshole, wanting to relive the family picnics of old. Heck, who was she kidding? She'd brought it up; she'd planted the idea in Roth's head. Sure, she could use working the next day as an excuse, but it was a lame one. There'd been many a day lately she'd partied until the wee hours of the morning and still walked the mail the next day. And what about the kids? They would go just to please their father. Would they get fried to a crisp? Be the victims of some phony terrorist attack on the Fourth?

"Kill me never," she said out loud. "Maybe I *should* have let the shrink prescribe me Prozac! I think I'm going nuts here!"

"Not too far a drive, Mom?"

Josh had been stalking her for the last two blocks as she walked home from the metro to Chad's apartment.

"What?" said Suzie, startled.

"Doesn't take much to drive you crazy, eh, Mom?" Josh said with a grin.

"Oh! I didn't know I was talking out loud! What are *you* doing here? Pleasant surprise!"

"Believe it or not, Mom, I was coming to see you. I took the metro down from Rockville, and we got off at the same stop, but you didn't see me. Surprise!"

"Well, cool, kid, good to see ya. What do ya say we catch some grub at my fave restaurant?"

"Sure, Mom, that'll be great."

"Well, come with me to Chad's, and I'll change out of these blues. Meet my new roommate."

"Cool, Mom."

The two had a strong bond, though they didn't see each other often. They walked in silence up the dirty DC sidewalk.

Josh wasn't the only one to overhear his mother's rambling. Clyde, the Galactic Guardian, heard *everything*, thoughts included. He really felt for Suzie. She was one of the diamond hearts. If only she knew it. If only she would ask him for help—even if she called him Jesus. *Just say it, girly girl.*

And she did. Silently. *"Oh God, help me through this mess."*

That was all Clyde needed. He paddled through the air up to his perch on the old tree and summoned his space buddies for a conference. Soon, the three of them were causing just a little more waving of the oak's branches than usual.

"Okay, kids, we got permission. Suzie's asking for help."

"What kind of help? Was she specific?"

"No, not really—her words were 'Dear God, help me out of this mess.'"

"Oh, good enough, but I wish they wouldn't mistake us for God. *Gawd*! What mess anyway?" asked Gretta.

"The mess she's in regarding the Fourth of July, silly. You remember, ol' Geronimo Jones and his clowns want to turn the Mall into a bloodbath and blame it on the Arabs. I think they want to pinpoint Iran this time. Great excuse to keep the ol' war machine going!"

"Leave politics out of this, Clyde. What's the bottom line? What do we need to do?" said Dorian.

"Well, for one thing, there's all those explosives planted in the grass…Hey, we'd better go to a safer place to talk."

Three barely visible twinkling silver lights swiftly returned to their invisible green ship.

▲ ▲ ▲

Josh followed his mom into Chad's place and cased the joint while his mother changed her clothes. No sooner had Chad introduced himself than he was preaching conspiracy to the kid. Preaching to the choir, he was soon to find out.

"Yeah, they're out to get us, man, but nobody believes it," replied Josh. "It's just too bad to be true! Who in their right mind is going to believe that our own government took down the Twin Towers? It doesn't matter how much evidence you show 'em, they have to cling to the solid lie. They say, 'Yeah, well, our government's corrupt, but they wouldn't do *that*!'"

Chad patted Josh on the back.

"You got it. But people don't change overnight. It's okay if they reject you; they'll still have that thought in the back of their heads. Then later, maybe they'll get that *aha* moment. But listen, kid," Chad started to whisper, "some of this is getting very close to home. Too close. They're planning some phony terrorist attack on the Mall during the fireworks."

"No *way*?" Josh's eyes got bigger than saucers.

"Yes, *way*, kid. Your mother and I—"

"Okay, I'm ready!" Suzie interrupted them. "We're going out for a sub, Chad. You want to come?"

"No, thanks, Suzie. You and Josh need some quality time together."

Josh gave Chad a puzzled look as he and his mother exited together. *What is he talking about? A terrorist attack on the Fourth? Now that's absurd!*

"So how you been, Mom?" They had slipped into the deli and ordered some sandwiches and a pitcher of frosty brew.

"Oh, I'm getting along okay, kid. Life's been kind of hectic lately, but I'm doing pretty well." She downed her mug of ale. It had been a hot day in the city.

The food arrived, and they munched in silence.

"Hey, my deli's got this place beat, Mom."

"Oh yeah?" said Suzie.

"Oh yeah, Mom. This Reuben's not even warm."

"Well, that's because they don't have a fine cook like you, Son." Suzie smiled. She adored her son and was very proud that he was surviving on his own.

"Hey, Ma, what about the Fourth of July anyway? Jenn's been texting me. Dad's been e-mailing—are we really going to do the picnic thing for old time's sake?"

Suzie's heart sank. *Think fast, Mamma-san! Think fast.*

"Yeah, I was thinking we could do the old family gathering thing," she heard herself saying. "Picnic baskets, checkered blanket, sparkly lights."

She couldn't get out of it even if it meant danger. If there really was going to be trouble, she was dammed if she was going to let her little shipwreck of a family go down without her.

"All right then, Mom, sounds cool—how we going to meet?"

She hadn't figured that one out yet. "Oh, we'll make a plan, kid. Heck, we can all take the metro down…Josh, hon, I might as well tell you. There's something pretty fishy going on."

"Fishy, Mom?"

"Yeah, kid, this sounds crazy, but I've got reason to believe there's something evil afoot. Something may go terribly wrong at the fireworks at the downtown."

"Oh, you mean you and Dad?" Josh laughed. "Always plenty of fireworks between you two!"

"Gawd, I wish it were that simple, kid," said Suzie.

Josh flashed back to what Chad had said before they left—a phony terrorist attack.

"Oh yeah, Chad was starting to tell me something about that. Seems pretty absurd."

Suzie cringed. Her roommate was already leaking the plot. But if anyone would understand and not think she was stark raving mad, it was her son. He had been preaching the conspiracy stuff long before she'd had a clue. She tipped the pitcher, emptying it into their two mugs and whispered the whole story to Josh.

"Mom!" Josh scolded. "You could lose your *job*!"

"I know, kid, but that danger's passed, and now, well, now, we really have to be on our toes. Hopefully, it's all BS, but what if it's not?"

"Maybe we should go to Grandma's for the Fourth, Mom." Josh's tone was serious.

"I don't know, kid; I just don't know. I'll figure something out soon and let you know."

The waiter took their plates and her money, and the two were back out on the street.

"Well, Mom, let me know," said Josh, as he disappeared down the escalator to the metro.

Chapter Six

President Henry Hush sat back at his desk, feet propped up on the monthly blotter. Deep in thought, he recalled the last secret meeting of the bigwig bankers and the higher-ups in the press. Population had been a big topic. The masses would be a lot easier to control when there were fewer of them. The planned epidemic in China hadn't worked out, but they were getting rid of a lot of Iraqis with the war. He wondered how many people flooded the Mall on the Fourth of July. Two hundred thousand, maybe? *Good grief, that'll be a lot of stinking bodies,* he thought. But Jones would take care of that. Good ol' Geronimo.

▲ ▲ ▲

Ellery tossed her graceful head back as she pulled out her driver's license and her credit card. Two pieces of plastic one couldn't do without at the airport. It was time to go back to Idaho to report to her constituents. Oh, she had a pretty good front all right—the doting husband, her two little girls, a modest house in the suburbs of Boise. But, darn, *We the People* were just a tad more perceptive lately. It was harder to pull the wool over the eyes of the sheep. That was how her dad had put it. And he was right. Why, on her way out of the office, she'd picked up a heavy manila envelope from home, jammed with signatures of voters from her state, demanding the repeal of the Patriot Act. No, the name didn't fool them at all. They'd be dammed if they'd let the cops search their homes without a warrant. On the back of the envelope was the red circle with the line through it over the stenciled letters: "Police State."

She wished she didn't know so much. She really did. If she hadn't had all her connections, she might not have realized that that was exactly the plan: a police state, martial law. Eliminate the chattel or at least turn them into good little robots. *So far, so bad, Dad*, she thought.

She was all too familiar with the create-a-disaster-so-we-can-have-our-way schemes of the Agloominati. And here they were, doing it again. The Fourth of July terrorist attack. *Good grief*, she thought. *What next?* Earlier that week, she'd almost tipped the page off. The sweet girl who scurried around the Senate floor. Almost.

Roth was following Ellery. Not an easy task in an airport. Impossible even, unless you too were boarding a plane. But he stood behind her in the baggage check line pretending to be a passenger too, just to see where she was going. But she was on to him.

She'd been on to him now for a while. She turned around, flashing her brilliant-green eyes at Roth.

"How's it going, Rent-a-cop? Tell Dad I said, 'Hey.' And, hey, soldier, here's a tip for you. Do yourself and your family a favor. Stay away from the fireworks this year!"

She tossed her head again, her tall, slender frame surprisingly strong as she walked off to the gate. Roth just stood there, jaw gaping.

"Next! Can I help you, sir?" barked the lady behind the counter.

"No, I'm not checking any bags." Roth slid his visa card into the kiosk to look busy. She glared at him only for a minute. He made a cautious about-face and found his way back to the parking lot. "*Report any suspicious characters to your nearest airport security. Do not accept baggage from strangers,*" blared through the air every five minutes. Roth felt his headache coming back. What the heck did it all mean? He couldn't figure out what bothered him most—that Ellery had found him out or her mysterious warning.

▲ ▲ ▲

The black Mercedes was parked outside a nice Tudor home in Bethesda. So were a bunch of other nice vehicles, a Beemer here, a Cadillac there. It looked like a party going on. Anzar and Mohammed had invited some "friends" over. They weren't too crazy about sharing the dough, but Geronomo Jones had been pretty clear about it. They would need the help of their dark-complected "brethren" that the CIA provided to pull this one off. "Not to worry," the old man had growled, "you will all be paid handsomely." Anzar was starting to wonder if the money was worth it or if the other half was even coming through. Or (Allah help us) if *they* would be just another statistic. After all, how could they expect a guy, an organization even, that was out to kill its own countrymen to be honest with them? Were they not just puppets in this big charade?

The women and children were sent out of the room and the men sat around a heavy mahogany table. Mohammed had an easel set up with a diagram of the Mall, the large stretch of land between the Capitol and the Lincoln Memorial. "Before Captain Mason gets here, I'd like to explain a little logistics."

He rapped a long wooden pointer on the four corners of the map, his brown eyes bugging.

▲   ▲   ▲

Good thing it was a Friday night. Otherwise, the neighbors would have complained and called the police. Mary Candy lived with her family in a middle-class neighborhood of mostly nine-to-five or seven-to-three working people. They valued their sleep. But tonight was Friday, and people were relaxing— out to a movie or vegging in front of the TV with a six-pack, watching the game, the race, whatever.

Candelabras graced the Candy's backyard at each corner, torches keeping back the mosquitos and lending a festive air. Two tables were packed with chips, dips, salads, burgers, and hot dogs right off the grill.

"Bring me the big platter, Mary. Looks like these burgers are done."

Jack Candy was proud of his little girl; he and Emma had been planning her birthday party for months. They went all out, within their means. They'd even hired Mary's favorite high school band, the Dead Soldiers.

Mary had a crush on John, the dreadlocked drummer. She was sophisticated for her age. Her long blond hair nearly tipped the end of her silvery miniskirt.

Mary's Mom, Emma, stayed in the kitchen, putting the finishing touches on the cake. She and Jack had invited a few of the parents over too.

"This way, we can keep our eyes on the kids. Let them party at the house."

"Enjoy being the watchdog while you can, Jack. Once Mary's off to college, zip, you'll have no idea what she's up to!" George Wright, his neighbor, knew all about growing young adults; he had college-aged kids.

Emma carefully placed the cake in the refrigerator for later, and went out the back door and stood watching the crowd of youngsters.

"Mom, *Mom*, could you not be staring out over the deck all night? For one thing, the band's getting ready to start, and you aren't going to like the music. For another, ah, Mom, it's a little embarrassing."

"I understand, Mary. Us old folks will lay low. We're going to hang in the living room and play a rip-roaring game of Scrabble."

Jack smiled at his wife, just as John rolled the drums and the band tuned up. A crowd of kids immediately gathered round, all facing the musicians and bouncing to the beat—nerds with glasses and "alternatives" with rings in their noses, all in a happy blend.

"What are you doing for the Fourth?" Mary grabbed Josh during the break, eying John to see if he would be jealous.

"Oh, I think we're going down to the Mall for the fireworks—a family picnic thing."

"I thought your folks broke up?"

"Yeah, they did." Josh shrugged. "Wonders never cease." But Mary Candy wasn't listening; she was already moving through the crowd.

▲ ▲ ▲

The Galactic Guardians had peeked in on the party. They loved watching people have a good time. And they were crazy about the Dead Soldiers' songs, especially the line, "*Peace, peace, peace, peace, when's this world gonna ever find peace?*" They were all about peace. Their civilization looked with disbelief and horror at the perpetual violence on Earth, and other primitive planets. But they realized that their human counterparts were still evolving, teenagers, all of them, just like the kids at the party. Their biggest concern was whether these adolescent Earth humans would survive long enough to grow up. In general, the Guardians just had to let things be, since Earth was a free-will planet, but when it came to nuclear weapons and nuclear power plants even, they'd been given the go-ahead to thwart things. Planet Earth was just too precious a place to go up in smoke. It would throw the whole galaxy out of whack. So Source Master allowed the many Galactic Guardians, including Clyde and his friends, a limited amount of power.

Tonight, a group of twelve of them sat around a large translucent table resting on a cloud, far beyond Mary's party. They had a lot on the agenda. Protect Suzie; protect Chad; protect Josh; tweak in on Anzar's and Mohammed's thoughts; keep up with Ellery; and in general, just send down loving beams of light to the blue-green world below. But it wasn't all that simple. Their light was bright, but sometimes it just bounced back. The darkness of hatred and fear was a pretty thick soup.

"This meeting will now come to order!" rang out the melodious voice of Phoebe, angel-in-charge of the DC Metropolitan District of Earth.

"Our main issue tonight, Sisters and Brothers, as you well know, is the coming Fourth of July celebration at the DC Mall. It doesn't look great right now, but things can change. Clyde, Gretta, and Dorian have been gathering the facts. Clyde, you have the floor."

Clyde stood quickly to his feet. He was proud to be the spokesman in this gathering, which was largely attended by strong, beautiful, and ageless females.

"Well, folks, the Agloominati are at it again. They're planning another mass murder, as if they didn't have enough of them already. The powers that be are planning to burn up the Fourth of July party in DC. Then they plan to blame it on Muslim terrorists. And like Phoebe said, it doesn't look too good. Just like in Iraq, Afghanistan, and the Gulf oil spill, some of the more recent events, we just don't have the authority to stop it. It's a free-will planet, you know."

"Get to the point, Clyde. You can at least tell us about the players," Penelope, dressed in a sparkling white robe, piped in.

"Well, we've got Suzie, the mail lady who inter-cepted a letter telling of the attack. We've got her roommate, Chad, who'll be spreading the news. We've got Suzie's whole family to protect. They're all in quite a bit of danger. Another person we must watch over, who may go out of the area, is Ellery Rocker; she's getting ready to defect. But the plan is in place, my friends, and frankly, I really don't know what to do!"

Suzie's guardian angel, Patrick, piped in, "I've got her covered, you guys, and her family too. She's thinking twice about the picnic she planned. They're not going to go through with it. She's pretty thick-headed, but I've knocked a little sense into her."

"Okay, okay, what about the others?" Phoebe asked.

Chad's guide, Flora, offered, "Well, really, I tell you, Chad is pretty tired of this incarnation. He wants to move on. They plan to kill him, and they will succeed. His soul group is already planning a welcome-home party."

"Woohoo!" the whole crowd murmured in delight.

"And Ellery?"

"Ellery's well out of danger, on the Fourth anyway; she's already gone back to Idaho. But her father's in a tizzy; he can't control her!" said Gretta. "Who, John D.?"

"Yeah, John D. Rocker's a hard one. Hard core, bent on the New World Order and all that. But he loves his daughter. He's been hitting the bourbon a lot lately."

"Thanks, Gretta. You'll just have to watch and wait."

More and more suggestions were passed across the glowing green table, and finally, the meeting was adjourned.

Chapter Seven

Suzie was chain-smoking and pacing the floor too. Thursday July 3. Was it the night before doomsday? She'd already downed three of the beers in her six-pack, and Chad had offered her some weed. Boy, did she need it! She needed every one of her habits to muster up the courage to face tomorrow. Her thoughts raced. Another fancy letter from Chicago had come today, but she doubted it would be read by the president anytime soon. The White House had been suspiciously quiet today.

Then suddenly, she came to her senses. She would change the plans! After all, they were always welcome at her ex-in-laws'. She couldn't stand Roth's sister or mother either; what a hell she had endured with the Morgans. The wounds were still sore, and of course, they were against the divorce.

But still, they were gracious and hospitable people. Their elegant home sat on a hill in what was left of the country–far removed from the pentangle-shaped city. They loved her kids and always gave them each a big check for Christmas. The whole gang would be there. They would blend. *We could just say we heard there was going to be a terrorist attack on the Mall. Yeah, right, Suzie, that would go over real big.*

But it was definitely the lesser of two evils. Why take a chance? She could drop by the deli and buy some potato salad. She'd have to call Roth and quick—and the kids. It just wasn't worth it, putting the family in danger. It wasn't too late to change the plan. She dialed Ethel Roth. Manners were manners.

▲ ▲ ▲

Jenn sat back on her long, thin dorm bed, eyeing the stack of books on the end table. She wasn't fond of cracking the books on a holiday, but she'd rather study than participate in the phony picnic thing her estranged parents had planned for tomorrow. Who did they think she was anyway, a stupid child? Sorry, folks, the damage had been done. No turning back the clock for her. She was twenty years old but felt forty. She was in no mood to put up a front for the folks. But she would. Just for the folks. At least brother would be there.

Her cell phone flashed. Think of the devil. A text from her twin brother Josh in all capitals: "*SOMETHING FISHY BOUT TOMORROW. WORSE THAN THE FAM SCENE.*" What the heck was he talking about? Josh liked to think he was psychic, and dammit, thought Jenn, sometimes he was! Was this a new twist of fate? Maybe she would get out of it after all.

"WTF R U talkin about?"

"Not just feelings, sis, clues too"

"Clues? What?"

"Not wanna text about it"

"Well come over here! U can spend nite in dorm &
we'll leave together in am"

"OK see you soon."

Jenn opened her anatomy book. She'd take the next half hour to study before her brother arrived. What a relief! At least Josh would understand her ambivalence about tomorrow. They'd tackle their wacko parents together. And whatever else. She took a deep breath and got out the highlighter.

▲ ▲ ▲

One more thing before he left to rescue his sister from the emotional frying pan. Call Dad. Give him a clue. Get his take on all this. Josh would be damned if he was going to let his mom, dad, and sister walk willingly into a burning hell.

"Hello, Dad."

"Hello, Son." Roth picked up the landline, the ring echoing through the empty house.

"What's up, Son? You ready for tomorrow's picnic?"

"That's what I called about, Dad."

Silence.

"Hey, I want to get together with Mom and Jenn and all, but I dunno about down at the Mall." Josh swallowed air and a chunk of pride. "Frankly, I'm a little worried, Dad. Mom said she'd seen a letter to the White House from some guy in Chicago about a terrorist attack at the fireworks."

"What? She stole a letter?" Roth yelled. "That's absolutely crazy, kid; your mother's gone off the deep end! And besides, if she supposedly knows about some goddamn terrorist attack plan, why the hell is she going through with plans for the picnic?" Suddenly, Roth remembered Ellery's mysterious notes and her warning at the airport, when she turned and caught him. But he said nothing.

"Mom *is* a little nuts, Dad, I agree. But if there's any truth to it at all, why risk it?"

Roth wanted to say, "Do as you're told, Son. See you tomorrow," and slam down the phone. But he his authority had vanished.

"Look, Dad, think it over, huh? We can still have our picnic—just maybe not downtown. I'll call you later, okay?"

"Yeah, okay."

Roth turned the TV up and sank down into his lonely easy chair. He made the mental note to review the pics of Ellery's papers from that curious day at the Capitol. The phone rang again. Damn, twice in a row! This time, it was the ex.

"Hello?"

"Hello, Roth; it's Suzie."

"Hey, what's up?"

"I just got off the phone with your mom. Listen, Roth, this whole picnic thing's getting crazy. We can't go down to the Mall. Your mom was happy to hear from me—she said we're more than welcome up at their place for the Fourth."

Roth's stomach took a turn. Great. How embarrassing, after the divorce, to show up at the folks' with the ex. His relationship with his parents had always been fragile, but now it was worse. They were all about "family," and he'd failed royally at keeping his little tribe together. He managed to grunt out, "How's Mom doing?"

"She sounded fine, Roth. They're having the usual barbecue out back. Jilly will be there. And Charles, and all the kids. You know I'm not that crazy about going up there, but we can't go down to the Mall."

"Why not?" Roth feigned ignorance. He wanted to hear Suzie stumble through her explanation.

"You're not going to believe me—I don't think I should even tell you. It's crazy."

"Try me."

"Well, what it is, Roth, is there might be more than fireworks tomorrow. They're planning a fake terrorist attack."

Roth grinned. He still loved putting Suzie on the spot.

"Oh, really? Sounds pretty bizarre if you ask me, Suzie."

Pause. Silence on the other end. Suzie was hitting a joint.

"But I had the sandwiches all made. Even got some pink lemonade."

More silence. Roth decided to open up.

"Josh just called me too. He doesn't want to go downtown either."

"So he told you the story?" said Suzie. How like her ex, to let her make a fool of herself.

"Yeah, he told me all about this *supposed* terrorist attack," said Roth.

"Okay, it's settled then. We're changing the plan. We're going up to your folks'."

"If you say so, dear. You want me to drive?"

"Yeah, I'll pick up the kids at college, and bring them to our, er, your place at two, and you can drive us up there."

"Fine. Okay. See you tomorrow."

Roth hung up. Same old thing. Being bossed around by the wife—er—ex-wife. He really would have rather done the separate picnic thing at the Mall. Now it was getting complicated.

The phone rang again. This time, it was his mother, all smooth and buttery.

"Hello, Roth. So you guys are coming for the Fourth after all. It will be nice to see you. Your father will be pleased. I'm glad you're not going into DC, so many undesirables down there. Didn't you tell me earlier that you and Suzie and the kids were going to the Mall?"

"Yes, Mother."

"What made you change your plans?"

"Suzie changed her mind."

▲ ▲ ▲

Flipping her cell closed, Suzie breathed a sigh of relief. She stepped out of her bedroom to face

Chad, who was pacing the floor. He was not a happy camper.

"We're not going to the Mall tomorrow. Too risky."

"Oh, so that makes it all better then, eh?" Chad was livid. Who the hell did she think she was?

"Now that you and your precious family are out of danger, everything's just peachy, right? What about the thousands of innocent people who don't know what you know? You just want to hold on to your little secret? Look, Miss Priss Mail Lady, we don't have to give you away. But we have to tell people!"

"But they'll think we're nuts!"

"Leave it to me, girly. I'll take the rap. I don't give a rat's ass what people think. What if you'd known about 9/11? Would you have watched three thousand people go down just because you didn't want to be called crazy?"

Suzie had never seen Chad this mad. He'd always been Mr. Kind-Considerate-Blasé. Not tonight—he stood, hands on hips, foot tapping an angry rhythm, his eyes shooting darts.

"Listen, girl, I'm putting it up on YouTube. I'm sending out a mass e-mail. I'm calling all my friends! Isn't there something in your goddamn Holy Bible about sins of omission?"

Chad was growling now. Suzie was shaking. She hadn't picked up a Bible in years.

"I'm going outside to smoke. I'll be back."

Chad yanked his yellow locks and let out a long, silent scream. He drew in a long, deep breath, and suddenly, he was calm. Perfectly calm. Suzie's cell phone rang. It was Josh. Chad picked it up.

"What are we gonna do, Josh?"

"You tell me, Mr. Whistleblower."

Suzie tiptoed back in the front door.

"I've got a plan, son. Get me on the computer."

"Okay, let me talk to Mom."

Chad handed her the phone. "It's Josh."

"Hi, kid, well, I just talked to Dad."

"Oh yeah?"

"I've changed my mind, Josh. We're going up to Grandma's tomorrow. Listen, kid, I'm exhausted. Tell Jenn. I'll call you first thing in the morning."

"Okay, Mom, good deal." They hung up.

"Chad, I've got to crash."

"I know; you rest. Didn't mean to be so hard on you." He almost gave her a hug. She was too wiped out to notice his change of heart; she grabbed two beers and brought them into her room. Five minutes later, she was dead to the world.

▲ ▲ ▲

Chad and Josh messaged back and forth online. What could they do? How could they reach the people at such a late hour? They certainly couldn't broadcast, "Agloominati plans fake terrorist attack." Or could they? That's exactly what they decided to do, minus the words *Agloominati and fake.* Chad powdered his face, fluffed his hair, and turned his webcam to record, his painting of the American flag behind him. *"Good evening, fellow citizens of the United States. This is a warning video. I have reason to believe, from an anonymous source, that there will be a terrorist attack tomorrow at the Fourth of July fireworks in Washington DC. My advice is for DC residents is to stay clear of the Mall tomorrow, or at least proceed with extreme caution. I cannot reveal my sources for safety reasons. I am taking a risk myself here, folks."* He made his best handsome frown. *"I repeat. Possible calamity tomorrow at the fireworks in downtown DC! Stay away from the Mall tomorrow!"*

A click or two and it was on his YouTube channel. Another click and it was up on Facebook. He didn't care. He looked like an idiot, but he didn't care. He sent it to Josh.

"What do you think?" he messaged.

Josh was right there. He took a few minutes to watch Chad's video and replied, "Not bad, my friend, but wait till you see mine! I'm still composing. Will send when I'm done."

"OK," typed Chad.

He still had some other places to send his video, including Felix Drones at Captive Earth. He even thought of calling the TV stations. He hadn't made up his mind about that yet.

Josh's video was words on the screen in red capitals, overlapping a picture of the Washington Monument, with Stevie Ray Vaughn's wiped-out version of the national anthem in the background.

ATTENTION, DC RESIDENTS! THE BEAST
IS KNOCKING AT YOUR DOOR. PLANNED

TERRORIST ATTACK AT THE FIREWORKS TOMORROW JULY 4TH PLEASE DON'T GO. IF YOU VALUE YOUR LIFE, RETREAT! THIS IS NOT A HOAX!!! MOTHERS, FATHERS, SISTERS, BROTHERS, TAKE YOUR PICNIC ELSEWHERE!! PLEASE PASS THIS ON! PASS THIS ON!

Josh posted his video on Facebook and YouTube, besides sending it directly to a bunch of his friends. His band buddy Robert, e-mailed him back, "Have you lost your mind, dude? Do you want the Feds on your back?" Yeah, Josh had thought of that. Ha, ha, freedom of speech, what a joke! They were already watching him anyway. Give them something to talk about. Give the poor suckers some excitement.

He called his twin sister.

"I'm coming, Jenn. Got delayed a little." He wanted to tell her, "Check out my Facebook page," but he knew how she'd react. It could wait. "Well, hurry already," said Jennifer. The anatomy was making her head swim.

▲ ▲ ▲

Chad went a step further. He called the media. He called the TV stations. He dialed the number for CNN. He thought about hitting star 67 to cloak his phone number, but he didn't. He got a recording. Press one for this, two for that. After fifteen minutes of circular motion, he finally left a message, "Please, air this immediately! Possible terrorist attack at the DC fireworks on the Mall tomorrow. Thank you."

He had better luck at the local branch of NBC. He got a real live operator.

"May I have the newsroom, please?"

"Just a moment, please."

Chad was starting to feel like an idiot with an unbelievable story. He was stepping out of his privacy box here. He barely called his mother, let alone TV stations.

"Tom Tinker, local news, what can I do for you?"

"Hello," Chad stumbled. "This is going to sound crazy, sir, but I have reason to believe there will be a terrorist attack tomorrow at the fireworks."

"You're kidding, right?"

"No, I am not kidding."

"Listen, mister, do you realize you could be getting yourself into a whole lot of trouble here?"

"Yes, I realize this."

"What are your sources? What makes you think this is going to happen?"

"I'm sorry," said Chad, "I cannot reveal my sources."

"How'm I supposed to write a story around that? Do you want me to lose my job, bud?"

"Dude, this is as hard for me as it is for you. I just want to warn the people."

"What are you, some conspiracy crackpot?"

Chad hung up. This was getting hairy. He hated looking like a fool, let alone a bad guy.

Tom Tinker picked up the interoffice line and got his boss. "Mr. Colander, some idiot just called and said there was going to be a terrorist attack on the fireworks. Thought I'd better call you."

"What?" yelled Mr. Colander in disbelief. Quickly, he hid his shock.

"Just dismiss it, Tom, probably just another crank call...Did you get the name?"

"No, but Julie might have seen his number come up on the caller ID."

"All right then, I'll look into it. Thanks for calling. But for now, just forget it, okay?"

"Yeah, Boss. Happy Fourth."

Colander was indeed shocked. He'd been at the secret underground meeting. He'd better tell Jones. Something was leaky in Denmark.

▲ ▲ ▲

Suzie slept, but it was a fitful sleep. Her legs kept jerking, and her head tossed from side to side. It was that reoccurring dream again. She was lying in a flowery field with Roth, all peaceful until the ground opened up and she was alone in a dark cave. She had become an old lady, and she was lying on a bed of smooth, cold stones. Then came a light, some kind of message. The light was tranquil. It was telling her to relax.

A loud chirp from the alarm on her cell phone jolted her out of her dream. She pushed the dismiss button knowing she did not want to wake up. She wanted some more of that wonderful sleep. She took a deep breath, hugged her pillow, and drifted back to the only place she found peace anymore.

▲ ▲ ▲

The twins had talked half the night, catching up on each other's lives. And Josh told Jenn about the change of plans.

"Oh man!" was all she said.

They fell asleep around 1:00 a.m.

"Brother, wake up! It's Happy Fireworks Day! Bombs bursting in air and all that."

Josh sat up, patted the top of his bed-head, and just for a minute, wondered where he was. Jenn's roommate was gone, and he'd slept on her hard dorm bed. "Mornin', Sis, where's the coffee?"

"We're going to have to roam around for that, my twin. Get up! I'm getting dressed. You'd better be moving when I come out!" She closed the bathroom door behind her.

He grunted as he collected his scattered thoughts. Oh my God, did I really put that video up on YouTube? Am I crazy or what? He hoped maybe he had dreamed it all. No such luck, he thought, as his feet reached his flip-flops. Maybe Mom is wacko. Face it, no maybes about it. But this is real. She may be nuts, but she's an honest nut. His thoughts bounced between, Oh shit, what have I done? and *I hope it helped. Maybe I helped.*

The twins walked in silence until they reached the cafeteria steps.

"Their coffee's really good here. Most everything else sucks, but it's surprisingly good coffee," said Jennifer.

They arrived at a dry wooden booth toting their coffees and two plastic-encased sticky buns. "Okay, what's the deal, Brother? What the *hell* are we doing today? You said Mom changed her mind?"

"We're going to Grandma's and Grandpop's!" Josh grinned. "We *were* going downtown but… Haven't you seen the YouTubes? There's a terrorist attack brewing!"

They both laughed. They had to laugh. The only alternatives were to cry or go nuts. Besides, they had to figure this situation out.

"You know, Josh, this is just a feeling, but I think the danger is past, if there was any danger at all."

"Yeah, it seemed so urgent last night, Sister, but now I'm thinking, it ain't gonna happen. But anyway, if it does, we'll just watch it on TV at Grandma's."

Chapter Eight

Geronimo Jones stretched his wrinkled body, as he peered out of his penthouse window. The Chicago sun was setting in the dust. Lake Michigan looked like the ocean. For a minute, he wished he were on the islands, away from it all. But not tonight. Tomorrow, he and his team would strike an alarming blow in favor of one world government. *Tighten the ropes, mateys! An evil terrorist is on the loose!* Maybe this was the final step. Maybe they would at last be able to corral the sheep into the cozy little concentration camps they'd built. His heart quickened with excitement. He knew their biggest weapon was fear. After tomorrow's massacre in DC, the fear vibe would be riding high. He buzzed for Millie to bring him his nightcap and the *Enquirer*, slipped off his jeweled Hush Puppies and his leopard robe, climbed into his poster bed, and opened his laptop.

One email stood out. It was from Colander at NBC in DC. "URGENT!" He clicked again and read the email: "Couldn't get you on the phone! Call me as soon as you read this! Very urgent!" Jones dialed the number. Ahh, the brandy tasted good as it slid down his throat.

"Hello, Colander, this is Jones, and this better be good!"

"Well, Mr. Jones, I just gotta tell you. Some fool called the station an hour ago trying to warn people about a terrorist attack at the fireworks."

"What?" yelled Geronimo, toppling his brandy.

"You heard me right," replied Colander.

Geronimo scanned his mind for possible snafus. "Who?" he demanded. "Who the hell called?"

"Chad Glass, some guy named Chad Glass. We did a background check on him, Boss, nothing. Just a gay artist guy living on Dupont Circle."

"That ain't enough. I want to know everything about him. Roommates, friends, haunts, the works. Get Homeland Security on this. Call Fred at the FBI. This was a no-leak operation. Damn!"

Jones slammed the phone down. He still had an old black landline phone. Perfect for slamming.

▲ ▲ ▲

Clyde and his small cadre of translucent beings huddled in the huge maple tree on the front lawn of Mohammed's home in Bethesda.

"Beam him a few more guilty thoughts, Gretta," said Dorian.

"I am! I am! Shut up, and let me concentrate!"

▲   ▲   ▲

Mohammed rolled over in bed. The wife was already up cooking breakfast. His bright-eyed little girl, Kashi, bounced through the door.

"Wake up, wake up, Daddy! It's the Fourth of July!"

He lifted his head, and it felt like a boulder had hit him between the eyes. What the *hell* was he up to? How many little girls would the explosions wipe out today? Granted, he disdained Americans, their hateful agenda, and their atrocities against his brothers in the Middle East, but did this justify the killing of innocent babes? And hell, even their redneck parents were innocent—ignorant but innocent. Blinded by their so-called patriotism. Blinded by their lying government. And he was going to make it all worse?

"Hi, baby, come see Daddy!" he said as he welcomed his little bundle of joy.

Just then his cell phone blinked and chirped. It was Anzar.

"Get online, man. Check it out. There's a couple of jerks on YouTube warning about a terrorist attack today!"

"Huh?"

Mohammed bounced his child out of bed and shuffled toward the smell of coffee.

"Just check your e-mail; call me back."

His wife was glaring inside, but she smiled as she handed him his coffee. She knew something was up.

▲ ▲ ▲

Chad sat on the cement steps outside his home, thinking. If he still smoked, he'd have had a cigarette. Instead, he took a deep, smoggy breath and looked up at the sky. *Now I've done it. I'm on every FBI and CIA wanted list. Homeland Security has probably beamed in my window Hi, fellows! What ya gonna do? Ha! Huh?* But deep down, he felt right. He was calm. He was not crazy. He had done the right thing. Granted, his YouTube warning and his phone calls were just a dirt road on the information highway, but maybe it was enough—enough to stop the bad guys in their tracks. They might not risk it. Then, boy, would he look stupid! Oh well.

▲ ▲ ▲

Mohammed took his coffee into the den and sat at the computer. Anzar had sent him a link. Some sandy-haired guy was broadcasting himself. "Ladies and Gentlemen, this is a warning…" Mohammed's eyes popped out of his head. *Now* what? Would they go through with the plan? This was supposed to be a top-secret operation! Who the hell was the leak? Yet, a sudden wave of relief swept over him. They wouldn't have to go through with it. Geronimo was sure to call it off. Better luck next time. He went into the kitchen for breakfast.

▲ ▲ ▲

Geronimo Jones paced the floor in a silent rage. What was he going to do? Should he risk being exposed and go on with the operation? Somebody *knew*! Who knew? Somebody told! Who told? Surely none of his close-knit group—they knew the penalty for leaking. Who was this Chad guy? Fred at the FBI had called back; Chad had a roommate named Suzie Striking, who worked at the post office—and delivered the White House mail. Oh hell! That woman must have intercepted a letter! Maybe more than one! Could they prove it? Get to the president before he shredded the letters! *Damn her! Bitch! She'll pay!* Jones cursed under his breath. *A goddamn peon mail lady. Thwarted our plans. And they were so airtight!* The colossal scream of fear wasn't going to happen. Not tonight. He was going to have to call off his plans for massive death. The blood would not flow tonight. Lucifer would not be fed. Damn! In his fury, Geronimo stubbed his foot on the corner of the mahogany desk. "Ouuuuuuch!" He hopped on one foot, holding his bruised big toe.

▲ ▲ ▲

Suzie was sweating bullets. The little—compared to the general population—circle of "truthers" on the

Internet was buzzing. Both Chad's and Josh's videos were being passed around from mind to mind to paranoid mind in cyberspace. The word was out. And she had helped. Heck, she didn't just help; she had started it! The word was out; the nation was warned. A possible disaster had been averted. She should feel proud.

So why did she feel so lifeless? Why did it seem like all the blood had drained out of her body? *No good deed goes unpunished,* she thought. A feeling of dread had crept over her; she could feel the eyes watching her. She'd heard about whistleblowers. Here today, gone tomorrow. Not a good day to quit smoking. She walked down to the corner deli and bought a pack.

*Okay…*Puff, puff…*Pull yourself together, girl. It's almost time. Got to pick up the kids. Then go to Roth's in Silver Spring.* Then they would all drive together through the country to the Morgan Estate.

▲ ▲ ▲

"Yeah, Dad. Okay, Dad. We'll be there. I promise. Me and Jenn are together. We've been hanging out. Mom's picking us up from the U of Maryland. Dad. Yes, we're okay. We'll be okay, Dad. Nothing's gonna happen." Josh put down his cell.

"Our father is…one tightly wound man, Sister."

"Ha!" Jenn replied. "With two such uptight people for parents, how the heck did we turn out so mellow? I guess we're just rebels, eh, bro? Comme ci comme ca, la ti da." A bomb threat on the Fourth? A terrorist attack? No way! All the worry evaporated away. They were children again. The world was their oyster. Their crazy mom would be there soon.

▲ ▲ ▲

Meanwhile, back in his hollow house, Roth sat in his recliner, eyes glued to the TV. He was on his fifth cup of coffee. A mugging in DC. A man found dead in his apartment. More troops deployed in the Middle East. A special on all the empty houses in Texas. He looked at the clock on the wall. A few more hours and he'd drive Suzie and the kids up to the folks' house. He, like millions, felt obligated to watch the news. The news was his thing. He thrived on it. It made his blood run. Action, action, we want action.

But he had to get up. Do this family thing. What the heck had happened to his family anyway? Just two years ago, the house had been filled with happy noises—Suzie in the kitchen fixing a meal, yelling some question to him. Whatever it was, she'd never let him just settle in and watch TV. She *would* bring him a beer now and then. She and he were so different. She hated the news. She'd shout at the TV and walk out. Those were the days. Heck, maybe he was better off here alone. No distractions, no nagging, no nookie. Oh well, she wasn't the only fish in the sea. But it would be good to see her. And the kids.

▲ ▲ ▲

Suzie honked the horn in front of Jenn's dorm. It was two o'clock on the Fourth of July. Her precious twins appeared.

"Hi, Mom!"

"Hi, Mom!"

"Hi, darlings, how are you? Did you sleep well?"

"Sure, Mom."

It gladdened her heart to see her kids; now she was sure she had made the right decision.

"So why the change of plans, Mom? Why are we going to Grandma's?" Jennifer baited her mom.

Josh scowled at her, finger over his lips.

"Well, it's just not safe down there, Jenn, and hey, I have the right to change my mind! I'm the mother here, you know!"

Jennifer just laughed and patted her mom on the shoulder from the backseat.

"I know, I know, Mom. Just pulling your chain. Grandmother's it is! Let's roll!"

The three rode in silence up to Roth's place until Jennifer said, "Hey, Mom, can I go in the house and pick up some things? I've got some good clothes in the attic."

"That's up to your father, Jennifer; it's not my house anymore."

Chapter Nine

Captain Bob Mason rose straight up in bed in the middle of the night before the Fourth. He never had dreams. He never had visions. But something woke him up, startled him. He rubbed his hands over his balding head and felt his unshaved beard. He froze. There at the doorway stood a hazy bluish shape. It came toward him, and as it did, it became a concentrated ball of white light, the blue around its edges. He reached for his revolver.

"No need for the gun, Bob."

The voice sounded like rushing waters.

"Plans have changed, Bob. No human fireworks this year. You will get a call in the morning."

The light shot directly up and disappeared through the ceiling. He shook Alice, his wife, out of a sound sleep.

"Did you hear that, Alice? Did you hear that?"

▲ ▲ ▲

Clyde steered the saucer, bouncing around space debris and circling stars, until up ahead lay the blue-green planet, the jewel of the galaxy. At least it once was.

"I wonder why Source Master gave those guys free will," Gretta mused, sitting copilot next to Clyde.

"Didn't work out too well, did it?" said Dorian, poking her head out from the galactic tunes she was listening to.

"It was an experiment," said Clyde. "Source Master wanted to check it out. He gave them all the tools, all the resources. And look at them now, killing themselves and throwing their garbage into space!"

"I'm glad we didn't get the free-will thing," responded Gretta. "We all live in harmony, and the rules aren't difficult. They are such primitive people."

"But it was the Lizards, wasn't it?" she continued. "Didn't they have something to do with Earth's demise?"

"Damn Lizzies, poking their snouts where they don't belong!" said Dorian.

"Well, deal with it, friends. We're in the Now. We've got to give Ellery a lift," said Clyde.

"We're taking her on board?"

"No, silly, we're going to lift her spirits. Remember the plan?"

Clyde made a left turn over London and skirted across the states to Idaho.

Switching to invisible and parking next to the driveway, the threesome skimmed out, unannounced and unseen by human eyes. There in the kitchen, they found Ellery Rocker, happy wife and mother. She didn't *seem* to need cheering up. Apron on, she pulled the bacon out of the refrigerator and the coffee out of the freezer. She enjoyed playing the role of a normal housewife, making breakfast for her family. Washington DC became a vague memory.

It had been so sweet, reading Emily and Patricia bedtime stories last night. The quiet Idaho evening. Looking out the window through the lace curtains, the plains stretching out for miles, so peaceful. She had tucked the girls in. The youngest, Emily, had turned her head and said, "I dunt liked it when you go to Watinton, Mommy."

"I know, honey; I know."

Her husband, Frank, was the stay-at-home dad, when he wasn't farming, and he was a good one. But still Ellery's heart ached.

Bacon sizzling, the mild aroma of coffee hitting her nose, she reached back into the refrigerator for the eggs. The phone rang. The caller ID read *unknown.*

"Hello?"

A gruff, deep, muffled male voice answered, "We know what you're thinking, Miss Rocker. And we don't like it. How much would you miss your precious children? Toe the line, bitch."

Dial tone.

Ellery stood paralyzed in the middle of the kitchen, and stared at the phone. She swayed, and nearly fainted, but caught herself, gripping the cold countertop of the center island.

"Well, she needs cheering up now!" Dorian said as she looked with alarm at Gretta. The invisibles had been perched near the ceiling in a corner of the kitchen.

"Protect her thoughts."

They immediately sent the electric blue ray of protection around Ellery's head. But the light bounced right back. Ellery's fear vibe had shot up to 100 percent. She stumbled down the hall to the children's room, arms outstretched, steadying herself against the walls. There they were, still asleep, the lights of her life, her two little girls. She sighed a hesitant sigh of relief and ran to Frank, who had just sat up in bed and was rubbing the sand out of his eyes.

"Frank, hold me."

"You're shivering, honey."

All her morning joy was gone, melted away. She sobbed and sobbed as Frank wrapped his arms around her and patted her head.

"What is it, honey?"

Frank's deep-set eyes pierced right through her tear-covered ones.

"The kids, the kids, they've threatened the kids! Oh, God, Frank, this is too terrible! I can't do it! I can't do it! They *know* I want out of it. I can't move one *inch* out of Daddy's cage or I'll get slammed. I wouldn't put it past them to kill the kids."

More sobs.

"Don't sweat, Ellery. We've got today, don't we? What's that smell? Is something burning?"

"Oh no, the bacon!"

She ran to the kitchen and turned off the stove. Rushing back to Frank, she was now sober and determined. "I was getting out of line, Frankie, wanting the flat tax and to take some money out of defense for education. No can do. I've just got to keep up my act. I'd die if they took our children."

"Straighten up and stick with the Rocker tradition, honey. We've got too much to lose. Hey, is breakfast salvageable?"

"Sure, it'll be okay. I'll be okay."

She dried her tears on her apron and walked back to the kitchen.

Frank had hidden it from Ellery, but his blood was boiling. He checked the drawer for his pistol. He'd have to give the governess more hours. Damn those thugs. It must have been them on the phone. They won't destroy my family! Over my dead body!

The Galactic Guardians had stepped up to the plate. They'd called in a branch of Michael's army.

"We need a warrior angel at every door and window of this home twenty-four/seven! And double the guard on the children." Clyde had radioed to Central, and it was done.

"Shew, we were needed there after all!" squeaked Gretta as she piloted the craft back through the galaxy.

"Ain't no coincidences in this journey, Gretta."

Clyde was too shaken up to drive and sat back in the lounge, getting an infusion of liquid light.

▲ ▲ ▲

It had been no dream. Sure enough, the ball of light was right. Captain Bob Mason's phone rang bright and early at 6:30 a.m. It was John Dagger from the FBI.

"Morning, Mason. The gig's off. Orders from headquarters. There's been a leak. Inform your Arabs, pronto."

"What?" Mason acted surprised, but he wasn't.

"You heard me right."

Click.

▲　▲　▲

Squeak! The brakes squealed as Suzie stopped the old Jeep Cherokee in Roth's driveway. He'd been good at one thing, keeping the autos maintained. Now that she was on her own, she had the money, but she just kept forgetting to take it to the shop. The front door was open to the almost empty house. The rusty "For Sale" sign on the lawn was blowing in the wind.

Jenn hopped out of the car, followed by Josh.

"I'm getting my clothes, Mom; Dad'll let me."

"You coming in?" Josh asked.

"No, I'll just park the car out of the way and wait."

Doors slammed, and Suzie steered the jeep to the left of the garage, put it in park, and lit up a cigarette. Her mind flashed back to earlier times. It was okay when the kids were small. Roth had been a loving daddy. But, oh, the chaos when they became adolescents! He kept trying to jerk the kids around like little puppets, always yelling. *Do as I say not as I do* may as well have been his mantra. She should have left a lot earlier, scooped up the kids and gotten child support. But the thought had never even entered her mind. She put out her cigarette and breathed deeply.

That was quick, Suzie thought. Jennifer ran out of the house, carrying a stack of dresses and jeans on hangers over her arm. She popped the back hatch and laid them in the back of the Jeep.

"I was afraid I'd never see these again!"

Jenn was excited.

"Dad's coming, Mom. We're going in his car."

Next came Josh, carrying his old bow and arrows. He stuck them in the backseat.

Then through the doorway came her ex, wearing his short-sleeved red flannel and blue jeans. She remembered cutting off the sleeves of that shirt and carefully hemming them. Still good-looking, he appeared tired but hopeful, the old picnic basket in one hand, his car keys in the other. Why couldn't she just hate his guts? The same charm that had attracted her in the first place radiated. She refreshed her lipstick and got out of the Jeep.

"Ready?"

"Ready as I'll ever be," said Suzie. "You know how much I love your folks."

"Well, we could have gone down to the Mall. I was all ready, you know," he said, lifting the picnic basket.

"Yeah, I know, Roth. I know."

They all clamored into Roth's older BMW, a gift from the folks.

"Let's just get this over with, okay?"

"Yeah, Suzie, okay. Hey, by the way, you're looking good," said Roth.

"Thanks."

She felt a little spark. She smiled.

"The divorce diet worked better than all the others,"said Suzie.

"Dad, you made sandwiches, huh?" said Jenn.

"Yeah, kid, your favorite."

"Can I have one now? I didn't have much for breakfast."

"Well, I guess so. There will be plenty of food there."

"Who all's going to be there?" asked Josh.

"Not really sure, Son; your Mom made the last-minute switch. Probably the whole gang."

"Okay."

Josh wanted to say more; he wanted to brag about his video, but it seemed so remote and foolish today. Likewise, Roth wanted to spill the beans about Ellery. But they both said nothing. The family rode in silence, the twins feasting on peanut-butter-and-jellies.

"Hey, I've got to stop for gas; this thing's on empty."

▲ ▲ ▲

Anzar left his house and drove down to the pizza parlor, which was his restaurant. When he'd first bought it, he'd thought of making it a Middle Eastern place. But he liked money, and there was a much bigger market for pizza and beer in downtown Silver Spring than for curried beans and rice. He had closed it for the Fourth; he thought he'd be busy, but now he was not. He'd tithed to the Mosque, paid down the huge mortgage, and bought new tables and chairs for the dining room. He'd planned on sending the other half of the cash from Geronimo Jones back to the refugee camp in Pakistan, for rice for the children. That would have to wait. He felt bad about that, because, after all, they had saved his life!

And if that overweight honcho he'd met in Chicago thought he'd get his money back, he had another thing coming. Those Agloominati dudes had plenty of money, and he knew it. It was worth the five hundred grand just to keep his mouth shut.

Mohammed had invited him over for a feast, but he wasn't going. It was just too depressing, the whole damn deal. He wasn't at all proud of the plan to "fire up the fireworks," and he just didn't want to be near any of his Muslim brothers.

▲ ▲ ▲

Gretta, Dorian, and Clyde parked their invisible ship atop the Washington Monument about 9:00 a.m. July Fourth. They were ecstatic!

"It's all downhill from here," said Clyde.

"We didn't have to intervene after all."

"Well, yeah, for now, maybe; we've won a battle but not the war."

"Right, Gretta, but at least we'll get a breather."

Down below them were Chuck and Al, hastily clipping the wires they had so carefully placed a few nights before.

"Well, if this don't beat all! One day, we're setting up all this stuff; the next day, we're taking it down!" said Al.

"Hey, Mason is still paying us double time," said Chuck, sweat pouring off his brow. He wanted to light up a cigarette, but he'd left his pack back in the truck.

July days in Washington DC were almost unbearable, with the heat and the dense humidity. Chuck and Al got their job done as quickly as possible. But they missed a small section in the corner of the Mall.

▲ ▲ ▲

Roth's Dad, William Morgan, was high up in the DC carpenters union; in fact, he was so high up, he attended the national conventions. He was also a Freemason, thirty-second degree. Savvy about politics and world affairs, he knew just enough about the Agloominati to wet his whistle. Occasionally, he rubbed shoulders with some of the "Elite." John

Rocker, Ellery's father, and he had played golf down at the country club a few times. He liked to think they were pals, but Rocker was a bit standoffish.

Once, when he was really drunk, he'd confided some shocking information with his wife Ethel. He'd blabbed that the people who ran the government were only puppets; they took orders from a small group of rich guys. She'd only looked at him like he was crazy and told him to go to bed. He was glad about that, thinking back on his foolishness, as he lit up the charcoal for the evening's barbecue.

"Did you say Roth and Suzie were coming up?" he said to Ethel, who was standing on the patio, hanging Japanese lanterns.

"Yeah, they changed their plans at the last minute. They *were* going down to the Mall."

"It'll be good to see them. Too bad the jackass couldn't keep his family together."

"He's our son, dear, not a jackass. Try to be nice; he's going through a rough time."

"Well if he'd joined the union like I told him to, or come along with me to the Lodge, like the rest of them, he'd have a healthy income by now and could have kept his family in one piece. But no, he had to go his own way, flipping from one job to another his whole life."

Ethel just sighed. Roth had been an unruly child, disobedient and obstinate. More than once in his teenage years, they had bailed him out of jail. The tension between father and son came early on. Maybe it was because they were so alike. She'd put up with William in spite of his macho stance. After all, he was a good provider, and people didn't get divorced at the tip of a hat in her day. But she'd seen how Roth treated Suzie, and even though it disappointed her, she could hardly find fault with Suzie for divorcing her son.

Chapter Ten

Earlier that morning, tucked away at Camp David, before he got the call, President Henry Hush gazed up at the sky and took in the picturesque landscape, feet up on his favorite lawn chair, thinking. He was secretly hoping for the worst, hoping for the slaughter, for the "terrorist attack" that would finally end it all. Then he could usher in martial law to a soon-to-be-complacent and frightened people.

But he really just wanted out of it. He wanted it over with. He wanted out of his puppet position. He was so damn over it. Over it, over it, over it! He wanted to live in that fancy underground city the brothers had prepared for him and the others. But just a shade of doubt passed through his weary brain. Maybe it wouldn't happen. Could the people possibly become aware? Could his hypocrisy be revealed? No way. And yet he almost wanted to announce the whole deal. He almost wanted to give a new speech—one that wasn't written *for* him, one that told the truth.

"My fellow Americans, you are being deceived. I am not in control of this country. Neither is your Congress. Neither are you. The conspiracy theories are true. They

are not theories, my friends. Yes, it's true that a few very wealthy families control the whole world. It's a much deeper deception than you can ever imagine. My very life is in danger...especially if I actually read this speech...My fellow Americans, it's time to wake up, time to care about one another..."

He choked. He couldn't do it. He wouldn't do it. Too much to lose, and it was much too late. He didn't really care about the millions of dollars anymore. But he did care about his children. And his wife. He wanted them safe in the peaceful underground village while the surface burned. He could not change it. So why bother? End of speech, no can do.

He took a deep breath and stared out into the distance, quieting his thoughts. The angry squawk of a mockingbird protecting its young startled him. He lifted himself slowly out of his chair and walked into the kitchen.

"Mr. President, you have a phone call."

▲ ▲ ▲

Josh pumped the gas, Jenn ran into the store for a soda, Suzie smoked a cigarette, and Roth slipped his credit card back in his wallet, wondering if it would cover the next tank of gas.

"What're you going to tell my mother if she asks why you changed your mind?" Roth chuckled at the thought.

Suzie just stared out the car window. She felt like she was falling into the past again, into the years of playing the pleasing wife and daughter-in-law.

"Yeah, Mom, just tell her we didn't feel like getting blown up today!"

Suzie turned to look back at her daughter and son.

"Don't you say a word! They'll think I've gone off the deep end!" she gritted through her teeth.

"Just tell her we couldn't go another day without her delicious Waldorf salad!" said Josh continuing to tease. Josh hated Waldorf salad.

"Just tell them the truth, Suze: you stole a letter to the president, and you and your new boyfriend steamed it open!" Roth added.

"Give me a break, Roth!" said Suzie. "You know I have a hard enough time with your family! This whole thing sucks!"

"Want me to turn around?" Roth taunted.

Suzie just stared out the window. Roth was loving it.

"Relax, everybody, forget all the terrorist shit. We don't have to tell them anything. It's just a visit; we can all have a good time," said Jennifer.

"Right, Jenn, you're right. There'll be plenty of food and booze. We'll survive. Sorry, Suzie, but you're just so funny when you're mad," said Roth.

Suzie didn't think there was anything funny about it and resumed her silent gaze at the passing scenery. Jennifer turned her iPod on and jammed alone. Josh was hoping his crazy cousins, Clare and Bobby, would be there. Last time, they had sneaked out to the woods and burned a doobie.

Finally, Roth pulled off the interstate, wound through the quaint town of Barnesville, Maryland, and up a long country road, and they arrived. It was seven o'clock. Maybe about ten cars were parked on the front lawn of the Morgans'. Suzie picked up the cooler of potato salad, Roth steeled himself, and the kids ran on ahead.

Everyone was glad to see them—pats on the back, hugs, and greetings were exchanged. Mrs. Morgan didn't ask any questions. After all the hellos, no one talked a lot. The Morgans loved the television, and there was one in almost every room—the news in the living room, a football game in the den, and back in the screened-in porch, a movie was going. People separated according to their taste in television shows. It was their way of socializing, aside from the younger set. Josh and Jenny's toddler cousins played on the swings out back.

"Wonder where Bobby and Clare are at?" said Josh to Jenn.

Bobby and Clare were the teenage kids of Roth's sister Jill. "I'll bet they're back in the bedroom stuck to the computer. Let's go find out," replied his twin.

Sure enough, they found their cousins on the computer in one of the spare bedrooms in the Morgans' huge home. The monitor was bigger than life—a sixty-inch flat screen, mounted on the wall.

"Dudes, how you been? Long time no see! Heard about your folks' breakup. Bummer, man," greeted Clare.

Clare was dressed in a prim-looking print sundress, but she was anything but prim.

"Well, it was a long time coming; they're both better off now." Josh sat down in a beanbag chair and looked up at the screen.

"Hey, that's my band! We rock! You found my channel, man! The Dead Soldiers!"

Bobby grabbed the mouse from his sister and clicked.

"But what the hell is *this*, man?"

There up on the wall in living color was Josh's homemade warning video—huge red letters, warped "Star-Spangled Banner" playing and all. Josh's face turned as red as the letters.

"Oh, that."

"Yeah, what the fuck? Do you know something we don't know? You can't be serious, man! What is this? Some kinda prank?" said Bobby.

Jenn saved her brother, much to his surprise.

"Listen, Bobby, Clare, it's no prank. He's serious as a heart attack. It's probably not true, and to tell the truth, I don't really believe it, but he has his connections. Some idiots were going to blow up the Fourth of July downtown."

Josh had regained his composure. "You guys ever heard of the Agloominati?"

"Oh, something to do with the New World Order, the FEMA camps and all that?" said Clare.

She had recently been tuning in to the Captive Earth channel.

Bobby added, "I think I've heard of them, the goddamn Agloominiti. Skull and Crossbones, blue bloods, and all that. So what do *they* have to do with the Fourth of July?"

"Well, you remember Nine-Eleven? How it was a big inside job? The terrorists are within, man. This is the same thing, only different, man. They want to freak out the whole country so everybody will be just fine with a police state and martial law."

Jenn left the room. It was just too much for her.

"Well, whether or not it's true, dude, you've got yourself in just a little bit of hot water, ya know?" said Clare.

Bobby lit a joint, took a big drag, and passed it to Josh.

"Thanks, I needed this."

"You serious, man?" Bobby coughed. "The Aglaminty, or whatever you call 'em, were planning a fake terrorist attack?"

"A*gloom*inati, dude, Get it? G-L-O-O-M?" Josh spelled it out.

"Sounds pretty darned gloomy to me! Let's turn this damn thing off and go eat," said Clare, hooking a thumb toward the closed door.

"Do me a favor, you guys; don't mention this out there," said Josh.

"So *that's* why you guys came up here?" said Bobby.

"Just drop it, okay?" said Josh.

"Okay, okay, whatever," replied Bobby.

The three red-eyes sauntered nonchalantly through the living room and outside to the barbecue on the multitiered deck.

Chapter Eleven

The red sun had set over the sparkling waters of the pool in front of the Capitol steps, and darkness found what place it could between the street lights. Thousands crowded into the National Mall — mothers, fathers, grandparents, children, and groups of all sorts and sizes. Some spread blankets on the grass; some unfolded lawn chairs and camping stools; and others sat on coolers. Little ones gazed in anticipation at the sky above.

The pyrotechnicians were hard at work. *Zing* came the high-pitched noise that preceded a display and then a huge flower of white lights, followed by a *boom*. This was repeated over and over again, each configuration of lights and colors outdoing the one before. As the night progressed, the air grew cooler.

No terrorists in sight, and just a slight incident in a remote corner of the Mall. Two young men were standing on a blanket, downing beers and smoking cigarettes. One carelessly threw down a lit butt and started a small fire, which oddly ran in a straight line. They thought it was pretty cool, even though it burned a line through their army blanket. His buddy stomped it out with his Chuck

Taylors, before it could, well, *you* know, before it could do any *real* damage. A reporter happened to be nearby, filming the crowd, and it made the ten o'clock news. An amusing aside to the fireworks. No ambulance arrived; no security guards stepped in. There was just the putrid smell of wool burning, which blended in with the smoke and the smell of the fireworks.

And then it was all over. The grand finale came and went; the Americans returned to their automobiles, and the usual traffic jam ensued. The red taillights drew a long line up and down Constitution Avenue.

Clyde, Gretta, and Dorian had been hovering above the Washington Monument, ready for action, if need be. But all they really did was beam down invisible waves of kindness. And this did seem to help. Strangers talked to strangers. Drivers gave each other the right of way. Some walking toward the street even shared their chips and drinks with each other. Instead of a disaster, the fireworks ended in a small, barely noticeable miracle, the miracle of what *didn't* happen.

"Well, I guess we can rest easy for a spell," chimed Dorian.

Gretta and Clyde nodded as the twinkling green triangle rose up past the smoky skies.

Ellery, her husband, and the two girls spent a quiet Fourth. They invited a neighbor couple and their children for a cookout. The kids played with sparklers, and that was about it. The children were young and quickly tired, so their friends left early. Ellery kept the news on and wondered why it was so quiet.

Her father called at 10:30, ostensibly to wish them a happy holiday. But after the hellos and how-are-you's, he questioned his daughter, "You were at that meeting, weren't you?"

"Yes, Father."

"Well, what went wrong, then? I thought…"

"Doesn't look like anything went wrong, Father."

"You know what I mean!" His voice turned stern. "Have you been blabbing?"

"Why, no, Father, of course not. I know better than that," she replied as she remembered the warning she had given Roth at the airport. Surely, that couldn't have made a difference.

"Well *some*body must have leaked it," J. D. Rocker replied.

"Well, it wasn't me, Father. I know how to keep my mouth shut."

"Okay. Well, then, how are the kids?"

"They're *safe*, Father; the kids are safe."

"Good."

"Good night, Father." She carefully hung up the phone. "And no thanks to you, you greedy old bastard!" she added, glaring at the phone.

Frank heard that and looked up from his newspaper.

"I already hung up." She laughed uneasily. "He makes me so mad!"

▲ ▲ ▲

The party was still going strong at the Morgans' at 10:30 p.m. People had started to loosen up with the beer and the booze flowing freely, and only the living room TV stayed on. Suzie had been watching it closely. Just one little burned-blanket incident, very interesting.

Roth's dad cornered him in the kitchen.

"So, how's the detective job going, Son? Watching anyone exciting?"

Roth didn't take the bait.

"No, Dad, just a couple of husbands checking up on their wives and vice versa. Fairly boring, really."

J. D. Rocker had told the senior Morgan that his son was assigned to Ellery, but he couldn't bring it up without giving himself away.

"Just what are you driving at, Dad?"

William Morgan downed his scotch and water, shrugged, and changed the subject.

"Got any offers on the house?"

"No, Dad, as you know, the market is pretty slow."

Roth uncornered himself from his dad and left the kitchen. He found Suzie in the living room.

"Are you ready to go?"

"Oh, yeah."

For once, they agreed on something.

"You sober enough to drive?" Suzie asked.

"Yeah, just had a little chat with Dad—he has a way of sobering me up."

"Well, maybe you should have a cup of coffee."

"I'll get it on the road. Where are the kids?"

"I'll find them."

She found the twins on the back lawn. Bobby was strumming a guitar, and Josh and Jenn were politely listening. He was pretty bad.

"Ready to go, kids?" asked Suzie.

It didn't take much arm-twisting. Presently, good-byes were said, and Roth, Suzie, Josh, and Jenn were on their way.

They all made it back to their respective homes that night and all felt strangely content. Well, almost all. When Suzie made it back to Dupont Circle, as she sat down to rest, she slowly assimilated all that had happened. Chad had gone out, and that was okay. No noisy Felix Drones on the Net to interrupt her thoughts.

She was in a precarious position. She knew more than she was supposed to know. She wished for bliss-ful ignorance again. Why had she even opened that letter? But a little voice answered, *Because you had to save the Fourth of July, honey.* An unsung hero she was. She had saved the day, and nobody knew it. But that didn't bother her. It was the *knowing* that bothered her. Whenever some movie star or celebrity died mysteriously, she wondered if it were because he or she knew too much: John Kennedy Jr., Princess Dianna…heck, maybe even Michael Jackson. She didn't want to become a mysterious statistic. They would know. They would surely find her out. She was the leak. Ol' Geronimo Jones and his band of agents, they'd be watching her now. They'd be like that A.A. Milne poem about the bears—watching for her to step on a crack, waiting for one false move. One false, faltering footstep and she was a goner. *Mail lady loses life in one-car collision. Mail truck hit by falling comet. Suzanne Striking, recently divorced mother of two and estranged wife of Roth Morgan, becomes overwhelmed and overdoses on pain pills. Suicide note found by her pillow.* The obits flew through her head. What to do? Nothing. Just remain as visible and translucent as possible. There was no use hiding. Hiding would be even scarier. Then they'd *know* she was scared. No, she wasn't going to give them that satisfaction. She would continue being the goofy mail lady and look fate straight in the eye. She wasn't ready to die, but if the time came, she'd let it be known it wasn't an accident. Hmmm, that might be tricky. She would tell Chad; that's it. No, she'd write something. The world would need to know when she hit the sky, just why.

Oh my God, Chad! He was in worse danger than she. And Josh! Their stuff was all over the Internet, no doubt getting laughed at by the complacent majority and the media. But the bad guys wouldn't take it lightly. They'd be on her son like glue—and her roommate too. Maybe it was time to pray. She hadn't prayed in a long, long time.

Epilogue

Suzie died in a mysterious accident on the mail route. She was immediately greeted by Clyde and the Galactic Guardians, among others, with joyful pats on the back. Roth continues stumbling through the footpaths of life on Earth. Chad became infected with a scary virus and died in a few short months. Jenny became a nurse; Josh plays in the band and manages Big Dan's Deli. He slips through the cracks daily.

~~~

About the Author

Marie Suzanne Wasilik was born in Washington, D,C, in 1952. She grew up in the Maryland suburbs, and is the oldest of six children. She presently lives in Oak Ridge, Tennessee. She has two grown children, and two grandchildren. She is retired from the Postal Service, and delivered the mail in the country for twenty years. She has many interests and hobbies. One of her favorites is writing.